MISS MURDER

ZIA RAYYAN

Copyright © 2025 by Zia Rayyan

All rights reserved.

No part of this book may be reproduced in any form or by any electronic or mechanical means, including information storage and retrieval systems, without written permission from the author, except for the use of brief quotations in a book review.

For the Psychological Thriller Readers Facebook group: this one's for you. I'd say "sleep tight," but we both know that's not happening.

PROLOGUE

They call me Miss Murder.

But the only thing I'm close to murdering is the cursor blinking at me from the blank document on my screen. My hands hover over the keyboard, trying to flesh out words from the emptiness of my mind.

Just one word.

That's all I need to break open the floodgates.

But it doesn't come. With a frustrated sigh, I look away from the document and squeeze my hands in my lap. The walls of my office are lined with murder thrillers, each one a best seller and, most importantly, each one *mine*.

I shake my head.

With this many books behind me, how was it that I couldn't even manage a single word?

With a quiet curse, I click away from the document for the tenth time and go through my emails. I do any administrative work that takes me away from the one thing that matters: writing.

But when it's all finished and there's nothing left of an excuse for me to pull away from writing, I tab back to the document. It sits there, ready for a strike of inspiration, as I rise from my leather chair and stand before the floor-to-ceiling windows of my office.

It's a beautiful morning. The sun has painted the sky a portrait of reds and pinks and oranges. The birds chirp while swans swim lazily around my lake. It's almost picturesque. But not picturesque enough for me to feel inspired.

I glance back over my shoulder at the clock to check the time, but my eyes catch on the empty document instead.

The cursor blinks.

A familiar prick of fear stirs in my chest. I try to conjure an image—a face, a scene—but it's all static. My old teacher's sneer echoes in my mind: "You'll never write anything real."

My chest tightens.

What if the words don't come this time? What if this is the end of everything? I can hear the steady drone of my mother's equipment coming from the other room. The ones monitoring her health.

Somehow, despite that constant sound, the silence around me constricts, choking the air from my throat. I put my hands on the desk to steady myself, and pull at the neck of my sweater.

I check the clock again before forcing the thought away. It's the same every month. The words will arrive. They *must*.

Just as I start to sit back down into the chair and take

another crack at the empty document, the chime of the doorbell shatters the silence. I breathe a sharp sigh of relief.

Nothing bad ever happens when the doorbell rings. It's only when someone knocks that you have something to worry about.

I hurry out of my office and down the flight of stairs to the front door, where I see the mailman retreating to his van through the stained glass window. Once the sound of his engine falls quiet, I open the door.

There's a brown-enveloped package waiting on my doorstep, addressed clearly to me, using my real name of Luna Harrow. I pick it up, pleased to see it's about as heavy as I expect. The weight on my shoulders suddenly lessens, and as I close the door behind me, a soft smile plays at my lips.

When I make it back to my desk, I carefully slice the envelope open with a letter opener, taking care not to cut the precious contents inside. The scent of ink wafts faintly from the inside. I take a moment to breathe it in, recognizing it like an old friend.

It really *is* a beautiful morning.

I reach inside the brown envelope and withdraw a pristine stack of typewritten pages—another best selling murder thriller, I'm sure. I rest them beside my keyboard, neatly aligning the manuscript with the edge of my desk.

My eyes drift to the framed photo of my mother. Her thick brown hair was pulled back into a bun, letting the sun fall across her face. She had a radiant smile back then, her eyes glinting, so full of life.

Now, she lies in one of the bedrooms of this oversized

and dusty house, attached to a number of machines that beep and drone. With them around, it's easy to be reminded that without this money of mine to keep her alive, without all the success of *Miss Murder*, she would be dead.

I release a heavy sigh and run my hand down through my wavy hair. As long as the packages keep arriving this time of every month, everything will be fine.

The blinking cursor pulls my attention back to the empty document, continuing to mock me. My shoulders tense, but I force myself to remember.

I don't need to write. Not today. Not ever, really. The words will come.

They always do.

ONE

2 YEARS EARLIER

I have always hated hospitals.

The stench of disinfectants burns my nose, sharp and chemical, mixed with the sterile cold of polished metal. Even the air feels unnatural—too clean, too thin, as though the place has scrubbed away everything human. But sitting here now, wrapped in a thin blanket of my own arms to keep the chill at bay, I hate it even more.

I can't stop staring at my mother. She lies so still, so pale—like a ghost of herself. There's a hollow feeling inside of me. She's the strongest person I've ever known, and I'm not sure how I'm supposed to react, seeing her so... *broken*.

When my father died, she told me through dry eyes. She held me while I cried, whispered that we'd be okay. But I'd heard her sobs late into the night, muffled but unrelenting. Still, she was right—she made sure we were okay. She made sure *I* was okay.

And now, she's the one who isn't.

It's strange how quickly everything can change. One

moment, we were laughing so hard that my stomach ached from it. And the next, she's crumpled on the floor, her body jerking violently, her mouth slack and her eyes rolled up in her head.

The doctors gave me a long-winded explanation of her health, which if I'm honest, I didn't understand too much. All I got from it was that she wasn't well, and they weren't sure that she ever would be again.

I had no idea just how true that would be.

My heart throbs in pain and I bow my head for a moment, trying to hold back the grief. I've already shed all the tears I have in me, but my chin still quivers.

It wasn't just my mother's life that was in ruins. It was mine, too. Yesterday, one of the hospital staff found me and informed me that there was an issue with my mother's insurance. The billing specialist's words blurred into a meaningless hum. Deductibles. Lapses. Outstanding balances. I clutched the edge of the chair, my nails digging into the vinyl, as they politely outlined my descent into financial ruin.

Desperately needing an escape, I stand and pace around the room, itching to do something, *anything*, that would take my mind off the wreck of my life.

I pause when I see a pen and a blank pad resting on the nearby table.

Something invisible tugs at my heart, and a moment later, I'm back in my seat with the pad in my lap and the pen held to the ready. For some foolish reason, I dared to imagine that I could write a book; that I could write some fantastical tale that would simultaneously both pull me away from this nightmare and bring a bit of cash to the bank to help with the bills that would drown me otherwise.

It was a laughable idea. There were a few authors who made money off books, sure, but it wasn't lost on me that most authors lived penniless, and died penniless, too.

A grim chuckle splits the silence, and I can't help but think, 'Hey, I'm already on my way to being an author.'

But my chuckle falls away into the ocean of silence, and I suddenly realize... I *need* to write.

Maybe the need goes back to middle school, when old Mr. Thompson stood at the head of the classroom with that ugly sneer on his face and obliterated me for my inability to even *imagine* something worth writing.

I knew it was bad, because even the kid in the wheelchair had given me a sympathetic look after class. He might not be able to walk, but at least he could picture it.

I grind my teeth, determined to write something. But the words refuse to come, no matter how long I sit and wait.

A notification on my phone pulls me away, and with a heavy sigh, I set the pen and pad aside. I open up Momnt, the most popular video-based app out there designed to rot both young and adult brains alike. Habit brings me to doomscrolling endlessly, wasting away the hours of my life while my mind remains stuck on my own failure.

At some point, the doomscrolling stops, and I realize with a jolt that I'm staring back at myself through the camera. The app nudges me with a gentle notification.

Make a post.

I don't have much of a following. Thirty seven

people. Most of them bots, I'd guess. But even so, I hear the sound of my own voice, sharing the greatest tragedy of my life. It was punctuated by the sound of beeps and drones in the background.

Then, I made the confession that changed my life.

"I wish I could write a book, but I don't know how. I just want to help my mom." Before I could stop myself, I pressed post, and cast my video out into the ether.

The view counts slowly spill in. One person, two, then five. It slowly rises, and as it does, I wait for the flood of comments to come, filled with sympathy and encouragement. Everything that might temporarily fill my empty shell of a heart.

But they never do.

With a deep, soul-shattering sigh, I set my phone aside, hug my knees to my chest, and turn my attention to my mother.

Ding.

A heartbeat later, the phone's back in my hand. A message is waiting for me from an account named *Charles Dickens*.

I never liked much of his work myself. Still, I open the message.

I can help.

It's everything I can do to not roll my eyes. No doubt Mr. Charles Dickens is waiting for me to respond to his cryptic message, ready to pitch his pyramid scheme with the promise of unlimited money for little to no work.

People on the internet could be so cruel these days.

Just as I'm about to set my phone back down, I hesitate. What if it's a genuine message? Hell, for all I could know, a billionaire could be sitting on the other side of this conversation, happy to share a drop of his ocean of wealth—enough to hire someone full time to take care of my mother like she needs.

I glance up at her and a dose of reality pours over me. Yeah, right. Billionaires don't get rich by being charitable.

With a deep set frown, I type a quick response.

Hey, nice username lol.

I pause, shake my head, and continue.

What do you mean you can help?

I don't even have a chance to set the phone aside before I see three dots dancing on the screen. He was typing back already. Counting down quietly under my breath, I wait for the pyramid scheme pitch.

Would it be one of those ones selling knives door to door? Or would it be focused on the greatest makeup and skincare brands ever? Who knew, these people were always coming up with something new. Just the other day, I'd read online about a pyramid scheme over in the D.C. area where they try to get people to switch over to a different energy provider.

Charles Dickens's response finally comes.

I'll provide the words. You can be the face.

My eyebrows furrow into a deep frown as I contemplate the meaning of his message. What does he mean by he'll provide the words?

I ask him.

And a second later, *On the first of every month, I'll send you a manuscript. All you have to do is publish the book as yours.*

A book every month? The thought is almost laughable. What kind of madman is able to write a whole entire novel inside of thirty days? No, this had to be a scam. Plagiarize a bunch of work, get some money out of me, and then disappear knowing that I was left with nothing of any real value.

My lip curls, frustration beginning to spark into real anger.

I don't have any money. You understand that right?

I wait for him to tell me exactly where I can find the money to pay them, but instead, he says, *I don't need your money.*

My fingers pause over the phone. The smart thing would be to close out the app, turn off my phone, and forget about this whole thing. People always want something. If not money, then sex, and if not sex, then something far darker that will cost you everything you have.

But for some reason, I don't close out the app. There's something compelling about the messages. Charles Dickens was one of the most charitable authors in history, and for some reason, I have a feeling that whoever's behind the message knows that.

What do you want? I ask.

For you to be happy.

Interestingly enough, his message sounds ... genuine.

Why don't you publish the manuscripts yourself? Why give them to me?

You needed help.

I chew on my fingernail, the idea starting to worm its way into my head. It sounded too good to be true. But if there was even the smallest possibility that it was true, then it could be life-changing.

Of course, there were a million ways for this all to blow back on me and make my life complete hell, but ... staring at my mother, I wondered how it could possibly get any worse.

So you'll give me the books, and I'll publish them? How much of a cut do you want? My question hovers in the chat window as I reread the previous messages, waiting for a reply. Waiting for the trap to spring.

Three dots appear, pulsing with a rhythm that makes my heart strangely match their pace.

I told you, I don't need money.

You don't want a cut? I ask, surprised. *So any money I make is mine?*

Yes.

A chill creeps up the back of my neck. Nobody is this selfless—especially online. My thumb hovers over the block button, common sense practically screaming at me to stop this madness.

Just as I'm about to close the app, another message appears.

Would you like to see a manuscript?

What kind of book is it? I ask.

A murder thriller.

I stare at the screen, my heart thudding in my chest. Every instinct screams at me to block this account, close the app, and forget this conversation ever happened.

But then my eyes drift to my mother, her chest rising and falling in shallow, labored breaths. The machines beep softly beside her bed, serving as a grim reminder of how much time we don't have. The medical bills are piling up faster than I can pay them, and no matter how many late nights I spend trying to scrape together some semblance of a plan, it always feels like I'm drowning.

I chew on my nail, the bitterness of desperation curling in my stomach. What's the worst that could happen? I mean, really? I'm already at rock bottom. I don't have anything left to lose—except her. And she's nearly gone already.

The thought sends a sharp pang through my chest, and before I can stop myself, I've typed the word.

Ok.

My breath catches as I wait for something to happen. A reference for me to search on Amazon, a link to a document, anything. But to my surprise and deepest disappointment, nothing happens. The minutes turn into hours, and hours turn into days, until eventually, I forget all about it.

Up until a brown envelope appears at the door to my mother's hospital room a week and a half later, with my name written clearly on the front.

Inside is Charles Dickens's promised manuscript, typewritten in small font with the smell of ink wafting up to cut through the hospital smell.

Intrigued, I settle into my chair. Thrillers, especially murder thrillers, have never been my cup of tea. I prefer romance for the simple reason that I don't have any in my life. Well, that, and the fact that I don't care about dwarves and dragons and spaceships and whatever else.

But to my surprise, Charles Dickens's manuscript pulls me in hard and it doesn't let go. My breath catches as I'm drawn in by sharp, vivid words that dig deep and leave marks. The story gripped me so tight, I don't remember flipping through the pages. It's brilliant. Haunting. It's the kind of writing that people would kill to claim as their own.

And now, it could be mine.

It takes one sitting to finish the book. It took just thirty seconds from the moment I read the final page to send a message back to my mystery benefactor.

I'm in.

My heart pounds like a war drum while I wait for what's next.

His response comes a few minutes later. *I will send another manuscript next month.*

True to his word, another manuscript arrives exactly a month later. Then another. Each one is as captivating and meticulously crafted as the last. They come like clockwork, neatly packed in brown envelopes with no return address, and always smelling faintly of fresh ink. No instructions. No notes. Just a stack of pages waiting to be published.

But that first manuscript will always be special to me. It was the one that changed my life. *The Janitor* hit number one on the New York Times best-seller list and the Amazon store simultaneously, an almost unheard-of feat for a debut. And in that first month of release alone, it brought me a five-figure paycheck.

Everything began to go right for me. I was able to afford a full time caretaker for my mother. One of the best editors in the game approached me, capable of handling my quick turnaround, though she grudgingly admitted it rarely needed any changes. And I met a kind man, one I was ready to share my life with.

All of it—every last bit of it—should've been a dream come true. But I should've known better.

Dreams don't come true so easily.

It's funny how, when you look back, the things that matter most—the things that unravel you—are the ones you didn't notice until it was too late. Like how every package arrived without a return address. Or how the descriptions in the book were so precise, so real, it felt less like fiction and more like someone confessing their darkest sins.

At the time, I didn't let myself think about it. The money was too good, the timing too perfect. My mother needed the help, and quite frankly, so did I.

It wasn't until the knock at my door that I realized something was wrong.

And by then, it was already too late.

TWO

My reflection stares back at me as the hair and makeup team flutters around like moths, applying mascara, blush, hairspray—the whole works. Meeting my own sharp blue eyes in the mirror, I begrudgingly have to admit: I look good. Or rather, *Miss Murder* looks good.

At home, as plain old Luna Harrow, I'm far less polished. Never quite the stereotype of a writer in wrinkled, coffee-stained sweats—I do have some self-respect—but it wasn't uncommon to find strands of my wavy brown hair drifting through the air.

But none of that would fly here. Miss Murder needed to be the version of me people had built in their minds: a femme fatale with a killer instinct, beautiful with cold, piercing eyes. An enigma wrapped in designer fabric.

A knock at the door pulls my attention, and one of Alyssa Lake's assistants pokes her head inside. Clipboard clutched to her chest, finger pressed against the headset tucked into her ear, she gives me a nod of acknowledgement. "Is she ready?"

The question isn't for me—it's for them. The team steps back, their critical eyes scanning every inch of me like sculptors inspecting their masterpiece. Satisfied, they nod in unison and file out, leaving only me and the assistant.

"Ten minutes," she says, her tone brisk but polite. "I'll send someone for you. Do you need anything?"

"Thank you, but I'm fine," I reply, already turning my attention back to the mirror.

"Water?" she offers.

I gesture to the unopened bottle on the vanity. "Got one. Thanks."

She smiles, and I smile back, because we both know she knew that already. You don't get to be Alyssa Lake's assistant by being anything other than exceptional. She slipped out and closed the door softly behind her.

Finally alone, I let the mask slip. My shoulders relax, my spine slouches slightly, and the icy veneer of Miss Murder melts away. For a moment, I see just Luna in the mirror, tired but trying. The sharp pang of anxiety creeps in. But I know it will vanish the second I step onto that stage. It always does. I remind myself that while I might not be able to put words to a page, I'm the one who's published those pages and shaped the story of Miss Murder herself—the acclaimed and celebrated author who rose to such great heights from the deepest trenches of despair.

The knock comes again, softer this time, but it's not the assistant. It's Stephen.

"Hey," he says as he steps in, his presence filling the room with quiet warmth. He looks me over, a small, approving smile tugging at the corner of his lips. "You look incredible. I mean, not that you don't always."

I roll my eyes, but the corner of my mouth betrays me with a faint smile. "Thanks. It's mostly them," I say, gesturing to the now-empty room.

"They've got good material to work with," he says, crossing the room to stand behind me. His hands settle gently on my shoulders, grounding me. "You okay?"

"I'm fine," I answer, maybe a little too quickly. Perhaps I'm more nervous than I thought.

Stephen catches my eyes in the mirror and smiles. "You're beautiful."

"You said that."

"I wasn't talking about your looks, Luna." He squeezes my shoulders, his warmth seeping into my skin.

My smile widens and I touch my hand to his. Stephen isn't what I would think of as a conventionally good looking guy. Don't get me wrong, he isn't ugly, I'm still attracted to him. But it is his kindness that really made me fall for him. I'd never met anyone who puts me above himself the way he does.

He is the kind of man I could see myself living happily ever after with, even if he isn't the kind of man I feel comfortable sharing my deepest secret with. But that isn't his fault. It is mine.

Could you blame me though? Miss Murder is everything to me. If there was ever anything that went wrong between me and Stephen, that would be all the leverage he'd need to destroy both me and my mother.

No, even in the best of relationships, some things are better kept secret.

"You ready for Alyssa?" He asks, as though he must have noticed the slight drop in my smile.

It was a valid question. As one of the most prominent talk show hosts out there, Alyssa intimidated most authors. It wasn't because of the size of her platform though, which spanned the entirety of the online world from live TV to social media. It was because she wouldn't hesitate to obliterate you if your work wasn't up to snuff. And if there was ever so much as a *hint* of controversy, then you were in trouble.

But that didn't concern me. The skeletons in my closet were hidden well. I'd be fine so long as I didn't slip up about important details that readers loved about my books—details that most authors who'd actually written their own books would probably remember.

"I'm as ready as I can be," I say, holding up a small stack of notecards that I'd been studying while the makeup team worked around me. He squeezes my shoulder again, knowing how long I'd spent over them, pulling every line of every book that ever went viral.

"Good. You're going to kill it."

A small knock comes at the door, surprising us both. Had it been ten minutes already?

A girl pops her head in and fixes me with a look of urgency, almost as though she were afraid of letting down Alyssa Lake's assistant, who in turn would be letting down Alyssa herself. I'm sure around here, that would be enough to get you fired.

"It's time, Miss Harrow."

The mask of Miss Murder slips back into place with ease. I pass my stack of notecards over to Stephen and give myself one last look over in the full mirror. Whatever anxiety inside of me fades away as I take in the powerful woman before me, dressed in a blood red dress and black heels with a thin gold necklace draped around the neck.

I step out into the hallway, following the girl to where the mild roar of a crowd sounds in the distance. The assistant I'd seen earlier meets me, giving the girl at my side a nod, and begins to lead me toward the stage.

Head leaning in, she starts to pass off instructions. "Alyssa's doing the intro now on your latest release. There'll be a countdown before she announces you. When you hear your name, that's your cue to go out onto stage. Okay?"

"That'll be fine," I say, my throat suddenly feeling parched. "I did leave my water in the dressing room. Could you get me another?"

The assistant snaps her finger and inside of thirty seconds, I've got a cold bottle in my hand. I raise it to my lips, sighing as the water rushes down my throat.

Before I know it, I'm standing at the side of the stage, where nobody in the audience can see me. There's a small screen off to the left, highlighting just how many viewers are watching from all over the world. My heart skips a beat. Hundreds of thousands of people were tuning in. And that was just for now. Who knew what the final count would be, once this was finished and Alyssa's team clipped up the footage into bite size fragments for all her posts and reels and stories.

I turn my attention to the woman herself, resting in one of two luxurious white armchairs that occupy the stage. Alyssa Lake is as stunning as ever, dressed in a sleek navy jumpsuit that shimmers slightly under the stage lights. Her caramel hair falls in perfect waves over her shoulders, framing her radiant smile. Like me, she built her empire from nothing. Maybe it's the fake murder thriller author in me, but I suddenly wonder if she'd kill to keep it all.

"And it's no surprise that *Don't Breathe Twice* has shot straight to the top," Alyssa says, her voice smooth and confident. "Not just on the New York Times bestseller list, but in the hearts of readers everywhere. The twists, the tension, the utterly unputdownable narrative—this is storytelling at its finest."

The audience erupts in applause, and I feel a flush rise in my cheeks, even though I know it's not entirely deserved. My thoughts turn, and I wonder then if my ghostwriter is watching this. I imagine he—or she—is. After all, even with all of our collaborative success, this was still a big moment. It might even be the thing that propels me into the unheard of realm of seven figure months.

What I'd do with that money, I'm not sure. I have more than I can spend as it is. But at this point, it's not about the money. It's about the scorecard, how I'm faring against the competition. The larger the spread between me and them, the larger the moat for them to overcome.

Alyssa leans forward slightly, her eyes sparkling with excitement. "This book is a phenomenon. It's breaking records, sparking discussions, and keeping people awake far too late into the night. And now, it is my absolute pleasure to welcome the brilliant mind behind *Don't Breathe Twice*. Ladies and gentlemen, please join me in welcoming Miss Murder herself, Luna Harrow!"

The applause rolls over me like a wave as I step onto the stage. The spotlight follows my every move. It's hot and blinding, but I keep my chin high and my smile firmly in place. Miss Murder walks with confidence. Miss Murder owns the room.

The moment I take Alyssa's outstretched hand, her grip is firm, commanding, almost as if she is challenging my right to own the room.

"Luna," she says, drawing the microphone closer, her smile as dazzling as the lights, "it's so wonderful to finally have you here."

"The pleasure's all mine," I reply, my voice surprisingly steady. I thought I'd be feeling my pulse thud in my throat, but instead, I'm dead calm.

She gestures to the chair opposite hers, and I take my seat, smoothing the fabric of my dress as gracefully as I can. It's strangely quiet while I get situated, like the entire world is holding its breath for what we'll say next. And I imagine for some viewers out there, they probably were.

I'd heard before that I was the first of a new wave of authors, who were seen as celebrities and influencers rather than just imagined anonymous figures hunched over keyboards in dimly lit rooms. I was reminded of how true that just might be standing here on stage, staring into the camera lens and beyond, where fans were clutching my books to their chest.

Alyssa turns to the audience, her charisma lighting up the room. "Can we talk about *Don't Breathe Twice* for a moment?" The crowd answers with a round of cheers, the kind of applause that feels rehearsed but genuine all at once. "This book has everything. Twists, suspense, that ending—I mean, it completely wrecked me. And judging by how it's dominating the bestseller lists, I'm not the only one who feels that way."

I give her a demure smile, the kind that says thank you but also of course it does. It's a balancing act—gratitude without arrogance.

Alyssa turns back to me, her expression brimming with curiosity. "Luna, what's your secret? Your fans say your books feel like you're pulling these stories straight out of their own lives. How do you make your characters so authentic?"

I let the silence stretch for just a beat longer than necessary before I respond, letting the anticipation build. "I think it's about understanding people," I say, slipping into my practiced answer like a second skin. "Their fears, their dreams, the choices they make when no one else is looking. At the heart of it, that's what storytelling is—capturing those moments that resonate universally."

The applause is immediate, but it feels distant, like it belongs to someone else. In a way, it does.

"And that's why readers love you," Alyssa says, her smile widening as she leans forward. "You've captured something so raw and authentic and *honest* about the human experience."

The words hit me square in the chest. Real. Authentic. Honest. I've heard them all before, but coming from Alyssa, in front of an audience this massive, they feel sharper. Heavier.

A chill travels down my spine. My chest tightens as I force myself to smile back. If only they knew that I struggle to even picture a single one of my character's face. Or that I had a blank document saved onto my desktop for the last two years, titled *My First Real Book*.

A small voice in my head breaks through the veneer and whispers, *own the lie*. But I shove that voice back into the corner of my mind where it belongs. My mother needs this. *I* need this.

Besides, nobody knows the truth. And they never will.

"Thank you," I reply, my voice smooth, my mask firmly in place. "It means a lot to hear how much they love my books."

She turns her attention to the crowd, winking at them with heavy lashes. "And how much they love those serial killers, am I right?"

Another wave of cheers and roars surges from the audience as they shout their approval. I take it all in, the way that Alyssa molds this crowd as an extension of herself. It's a kind of power that has to be appreciated.

Alyssa laughs, looking back at me with a look in her eye like she knows exactly what I'm thinking.

"Somehow, you've made us all fall for the bad guy. How do you do that?"

Again, I let the silence stretch, letting my smile slowly spread. "That's the easy part, isn't it? Everybody loves a villain."

The audience jumps to their feet and they start applauding and cheering, and I know I said the right thing.

Alyssa transitions seamlessly into the next segment, praising my rise to fame, the book's record-breaking success, and the impact it's had on readers. The audience eats it up, clapping and cheering at every pause.

I nod and smile in all the right places, but my thoughts are elsewhere. I wonder if my mysterious benefactor ever feels a bit of regret, seeing how much success has come from their manuscripts. After all, even if they don't need the money as they said, it must still sting to see so much money going to someone else.

The thought lingers until Alyssa's voice pulls me back.

"Before we wrap up," she says, her tone softening, "I have to ask—what's next for Miss Murder? Can your fans expect another jaw-dropping thriller soon?"

I chuckle lightly, brushing a loose strand of hair behind my ear. "I'm always working on something," I say coyly. The audience erupts in laughter and cheers.

They all knew that another book would be delivered on the first of the month, and just like all the ones before, it would grip them in ways they never imagined.

The applause swells and Alyssa begins to shift into her closing remarks. The hard part is done. This façade, this carefully crafted image of Miss Murder, bestselling author and literary darling, is flawless as always. But I know the cracks are always there, just beneath the surface.

The interview ends with another final roar of applause, and I step off the stage, my heels clicking softly against the floor. Back in the wings, Stephen is waiting, his warm smile a stark contrast to the artificial glow of the stage.

"You were incredible," he says, pulling me into a hug.

"Thanks," I murmur, my voice quieter than I intended.

"You okay?" he asks, his brow furrowing slightly.

"Yeah." I force a smile. "Just tired."

He brushes a strand of hair from my face, his touch grounding me. "You killed it out there. Alyssa loved you, the crowd loved you. You've got nothing to worry about."

I nod, letting his words wash over me. But they don't quite sink in.

"Luna!"

Alyssa comes up from behind and extends me her hand, a thin smile spread across her face. I can't make out whether it's genuine or not, but I don't have any real reason to think it wouldn't be.

"You are a natural out there. Most authors are a bit shy in front of the cameras," she says.

"Thanks. I've had a bit of practice now."

"That's right. I have seen your social media. You're all over the place. You don't have a team, do you?"

"No, not really." I knew it was about time I got one together, someone to help me manage the newsletters, the social media, PR, international rights, and the million other things that fell onto my plate. But I'm not sure I could ever find anyone to trust with the success of my authorship. Anyways, without writing, I need *something* to do.

"Honestly, that's incredible. I admire you. I have no clue how you manage to even find the time to write, let alone at the pace of a book a month!" She laughs. I laugh with her, even as the hairs across the back of my neck raise.

Our laughs are cut short by the appearance of Alyssa's assistant, who begins whispering something to her. Alyssa's thinned smile starts to fray, emerging into a deeper frown. Something has gone wrong off set, if I had to guess.

She mutters something back to the assistant, before turning back to us.

"Sorry about that. I'm needed elsewhere. But keep it up, and I'm sure I'll see you on stage soon enough." She winks, then follows the assistant at a brisk pace toward whatever disaster drew them away.

Stephen and I stare after them.

"I'm not sure I like her a whole lot," he says.

I don't say it out loud, but there is something about her that I don't like either. Ambitious women are always something to admire, but Alyssa's ambition feels too sharp. Her words replay in my mind as she disappears out of view.

Keep it up.

THREE

When we get home, Stephen heads to the bedroom, exhausted by the long drive home. I'm tired too, but I don't feel ready to sleep. My mind's too active.

Instead, I enter my mother's room. The air is still, heavy with the quiet hum of machines monitoring her condition. Her eyes are open, fixed on the ceiling.

"Hi, mom," I say with a faint smile as I take the seat next to the bed. She must have been waiting for me to get back home. "How are you doing today?"

A soft sound draws my attention to the TV mounted to the wall. It's the same channel that my segment with Alyssa Lake would have appeared on. She must have been watching. Or listening, anyway.

"You watched the show, huh? What did you think?"

I don't wait for her to respond, knowing that she can't. Instead, I take her hand in mine, and press a kiss against her soft skin.

That same hospital stay that I had received the first manuscript, I had found out that my mother had been diagnosed with Locked-In Syndrome, leaving her conscious, but trapped inside her own body. In other words, she was incapable of speech or movement or much of anything, really. Occasionally, on a good day, I'd see the faint twitch of her eye. But today must not be a good day. She stares straight ahead.

It's a special brand of hell I wouldn't wish on anyone.

"I thought it went well," I say. "You should have heard just how loud it was, with all the fans cheering and screaming. Kind of crazy, if you ask me, but..." I shrug.

My eyes drift away from my mother, taking in the bookshelves lining the walls, two full shelves dedicated entirely to my novels. I've never read them to her for some reason. Maybe it was because I know my mother was more of a romance reader as opposed to brutal, gruesome murder thrillers. Or maybe it was because I hadn't written them myself. Either way, it just wasn't something I could bring myself to do.

"If she could, I think she would have been cheering too."

The voice is soft but steady, carrying just enough weight to pull me from my thoughts. I glance toward the doorway, where Vincent stands, his dark hair slightly disheveled, as if he'd just woken from a nap or had been sitting in the dim light of his little suite out back. He's holding a glass of water in one hand, a small notebook in the other, his usual tools of quiet efficiency.

"When you walked across the stage, her eyes were flicking all over the place. I think I might have even seen her mouth twitch," he adds, stepping into the room with a careful ease. His presence is calm, unhurried, the kind of energy that fits perfectly in the quiet of my mother's room.

I smile faintly, knowing that last part couldn't be true. Still, I look at her and ask, "Is that true, mom?"

Her eyes stare at the ceiling. But I like to think that she nods her head.

Vincent sets his notebook down at the edge of a small table, his movements deliberate, as always. His hands are strong, but gentle, as he adjusts her IV lines.

I watch him as he works. He doesn't have the cold detachment of a typical caregiver. There's something warmer about him. Something personal, like he actually cares. It was why I hired him, though I know Stephen doesn't particularly care for Vincent much. But if I had to guess, that had more to do with Vincent's distinguished good looks than anything.

"She's proud of you, you know. Aren't you, Madeline?"

My mother continues staring at the ceiling. At first, it took some time for me to adjust, trying not to talk about my mother like she wasn't awake or there. But Vincent caught onto that right away. I still remember something he said the first week he started. *It's important to remember that like us, she can still be happy or sad. It's up to us to help make her feel like she's a part of everything, still.*

When he finishes, he glances at the bookshelf as he takes a seat on the armrest of a nearby chair. His dark eyes linger briefly on the spines of my books, all perfectly aligned in order of release date.

"You were good. Really," he says.

"You watched the interview too?" I ask, a little surprised.

"Of course. I'm a fan just like Madeline here, isn't that right?" He looks at my mother.

Laughter bubbles out of me. "Okay, sure. You're a fan."

He's entirely serious as he says, "I'm serious. *Don't Breathe Twice* might have been your best book yet."

My laughter falls away as I study him for a moment. I'm not sure why I'm surprised that the caretaker read the books his employer wrote.

"Thanks," I finally say, keeping my tone light.

He nods, his focus shifting to my mother. Her eyes are beginning to flutter, like she's falling asleep. A few moments later, she does. It was strange when I learned that even staying awake can take so much energy out of a person, doubly so when they're trapped inside their own body.

I brush the hair back from my mother's forehead before Vincent and I quietly leave the room. He shuts the door, silencing the soft drones and beeps of the machines inside.

In a hushed voice, he says, "She was a bit tense this morning, but she seemed to relax once the afternoon hit. I read to her a bit. It seemed to help."

My heart tightens at his words, a pang of guilt cutting through me. I should be the one reading to her. I should be the one sitting by her side more often. But there's always something—another manuscript to review, another interview to make, another excuse to pull me away from the fact that I have yet to read a single Miss Murder book to her.

"What did you read?" I ask, trying to keep my voice even.

"Something light," he says, his smile softening. "A romance. I thought she might enjoy it."

That catches me off guard, though I try not to let it show. "You like romance novels too?"

"Not really. But you said she does, and this is my job."

"Well, even if it is just your job, I appreciate everything you do for her. And for me."

"It's what I'm here for," he says simply. "I'll get out of your hair. Give me a call if you need anything."

I give him a wave as he turns and disappears down the steps, retreating to his suite out back. It'd be smart of me to get some rest, especially after such a long day. But I just know that if I go to bed, the only thing waiting for me would be a long, sleepless night.

There are better uses of my time than that.

Once I change into more comfortable clothes and wash the makeup off my face, I pop open a can of Coke and settle down onto the sofa with the latest manuscript on my lap. It's not good for me to drink Cokes this late anymore. The small amount of caffeine in it makes it even more difficult to sleep, but I know that once I start reading the manuscript, I will want to finish it.

Wrinkling my nose, I take a drink and set the Coke aside, settling in and readying myself to dive deep into the mind of yet another killer. Since the manuscripts arrive untitled and without a blurb, I never know what the book's about. All I know is that one simple fact remains constant: blood will be spilt.

I turn to the first page.

As always, it's perfect. Each sentence comes without so much as a single grammatical error, flowing with such ease and simplicity that even middle schoolers could read them. Though I don't think that would be particularly appropriate, given the gruesome nature of the stories.

And gruesome it is.

The story of the serial killer begins to take shape, targeting a boy with disabilities severe enough that it affected the lives of his family. I watched through the serial killer's eyes as he peered through the window, catching the father bent over the bed, hands held together as he quietly, and guiltily, prayed for the good Lord to take his son peacefully and quickly.

My eyes drift to my mother's room, and I feel that same guilt claw at my insides. I wonder if I didn't have the money to afford a full time caretaker, if I'd be like him, bent on my knees praying for a good death for my mother. I push the thought away, trying not to think about it.

I turn back to the page, forcing myself to focus on the words. The killer slips inside the house with ease, as if it is his own. Chills rise across my skin as I continue reading.

It's infuriating how good this is. The pacing, the details, the way every sentence seems to wrap its fingers around my throat and squeeze. If it weren't for the type-written pages in my lap, I'd never believe this story hasn't passed through a dozen drafts or an editor's pen. It's the best book yet, better than even *Don't Breathe Twice*.

And I had nothing to do with it.

I set the manuscript aside for a moment, staring blankly at the coffee table. My mother's room is quiet now, the machines muffled by the thick door. I can't help but feel like I'm a fraud playing dress up.

I close my eyes, willing an image to form in the darkness. The killer. The disabled boy. The boy's favorite toy. I try to see it—feel the weight of the toy in the boy's hands, hear the soft thunk as it hits the ground—but there's nothing. No color, no shapes, no movement. Just the flat, endless void that's always been there.

You'll never write anything real.

With a frustrated growl, I grab the manuscript again, flipping through the pages until I find a scene that feels small and insignificant. The killer picking up the disabled boy's fallen toy.

The boy's toy is red.

I pause, my finger hovering over the word. Red. It's such a small thing, but it's also the only thing I might have control over. I grab a pen and carefully cross it out, replacing it with blue.

Blue.

It's ridiculous how my heart races at the change, how my breath catches in my throat. It's just a color. A tiny edit that won't change the story or the way anyone reads it. But to me, it feels monumental. It's mine now, this one small thing.

For a moment, I stare at the word, the ink smudging

faintly where my hand brushed against it. It's nothing, but it's also everything.

I press the pen to my lips, a bitter taste of ink and Coke mingling on my tongue, hoping that this could be the start of something bigger—something where I could carve out space for myself within these pages.

Of course, I wish I could write my own book. Really write it. But how could I? I can't see the scenes, can't conjure the faces, can't bring the words to life the same way these pages do.

So with this small change, it finally feels like there's a sliver of it that's mine. That blue ball will exist forever. I force myself to accept the fact that I could never write a book like this. But I could make it mine.

At least a little.

And that's enough. For now.

FOUR

The next morning, I'm waiting in a café with a cappuccino cupped between my hands and my finished manuscript resting on the table in front of me. It's not a popular place, though I don't know why. The coffee here is great and the prices are hard to beat. But I suppose it's not one of those 'trendy' places that everyone raves about.

That's the thing about marketing these days. If you aren't pushing yourself across social media, Momnt in particular, then it doesn't really matter how many Google reviews you have.

I sigh and shake my head at the state of the world as I take a sip. The time on my watch reads twenty-nine minutes past nine. In exactly one more minute, my editor, Janice, would walk through the door. She'd order herself a plain coffee, straight black with no sugar or cream, and make her way to the booth. She'd probably be wearing a long dress—a dark shade of some neutral color—and a single defining colored ribbon tied into a bun.

And sure enough, she does. I hide a smile behind another sip as I watch her order her coffee. This time her dress is brown, her ribbon a soft blue. Janice was a creature of habit, I'd come to realize over the last two years.

"Good morning," I say, setting down my cappuccino as she approaches.

"Morning." She slides into the seat across from me and pushes her round glasses up her nose. That, too, is a habit. I suspect it has something to do with the fact that they're a little too big and heavy for her face. She nods toward the folder on the table. "Is that the manuscript?"

She knows it is. She and I have our own little routine, and though it's rather impersonal, I can't say that I haven't come to enjoy it.

"It is."

She reaches for the folder, but pauses when I put my hand on it. Her brow lifts and she glances toward me. I'm breaking routine.

"Why don't you ever ask me what the books are about before I give them over?" I ask, suddenly curious.

She shrugs, making herself smaller and averting her gaze. "I like finding out as I go."

Janice's answer is simple, delivered with that quiet, almost apologetic tone she always uses, but something about it feels off today. Her fingers fidget with the hem of her sleeve, and her eyes dart down to the cappuccino cup in front of me instead of meeting my gaze.

"Fair enough," I reply, letting go of the folder. "This one's good. Dark, but good."

Her hand hovers over the folder for a moment before she picks it up, the motion deliberate, almost hesitant.

She flips it open and scans through a handful of pages. She must think me strange for delivering typewritten pages. I imagine most other authors in the world are more modern, sending over simple files, or at the very least, a printed Word document.

There's a subtle pause when she sees my handwritten edit. The change of the color of the boy's toy from red to blue.

"Last minute change," I say.

Janice's head jerks up, and for a moment, her eyes meet mine. Something flashes in them. Panic? No. Anger? Her eyes drop back to the manuscript before I can tell.

I lean back in my seat, my heart pounding like a drum for some odd reason. To steady myself, I reach for the cappuccino and lift it to my mouth.

She mutters something in a soft voice, just below the quiet hum of the café.

"What's that?"

"You changed the color of the toy from red to blue?"

"Yeah."

"Why?"

I hesitate, suddenly not nearly as confident about the change as I was last night. I clear my throat and straighten myself. I'm Miss Murder, the author of these manuscripts. Why should *I* be the one shaking in my boots?

"I felt like it," I say, with a sharp clip to my voice. I lean forward, my eyes narrowing as I fix them on her. "Is that a problem?"

Her fingers tighten slightly on the edge of the

manuscript, her fingers turning white with pressure. I'm struggling to understand why everything's so tense.

But all of a sudden, she blinks, smiles, and the tension disappears so quickly, I wonder if I was just imagining it.

"No. It's just a color." She tucks the manuscript back into the folder. She chuckles to herself in a low voice. "Besides, you wrote the book, right?"

"Yeah." I pause. "I did."

She gives me another apologetic smile. "Sorry, I'm not used to changes. You know what I'm like."

I push aside the unease of the past few minutes and settle back into the booth, meeting her smile. "It's all right. I'll try to keep from writing over the manuscript I pass you. Next time, it'll be typed in."

There's an idea. Type the whole manuscript into a document, word for word, and change what I want. I could have the file ready for publishing faster that way too, instead of waiting to receive the manuscript back from the editor. Besides, we both knew that there were hardly ever any changes she applied.

"In fact, I could start sending everything digitally, you know."

There's a stiffness in the way she clutches the folder, holding it like it might burn her if she lets her grip loosen.

"No, that's okay. I prefer doing a first pass on manuscripts by hand. This is better for me."

"Are you sure?" I ask, hoping that she might change her response.

"I'm sure." She holds the folder to her chest as she stands. "I'll, um... I'll get this back to you within the week. Like usual."

I tilt my head, studying her for a moment. After two years of these meetings every month, I'd learned that she was as easy to read as the manuscripts I passed her. But for some reason, I couldn't make her out today. Maybe *I* was the issue.

"Okay," I say, draining the last of my cappuccino.

Janice starts to go, but pauses, looking back at me over her shoulder. "What's this one called?"

"*The Broken Boy*," I answer.

She frowns, and is out the door before I can say anything else. I watch her through the café window as she walks down the street, her head down, her steps quick and uneven.

Was the title really that bad?

I debate about going after her and seeing if she had any better ideas, but I shake my head. That would be breaking the routine again, and there'd been more than enough of that already. The routines and systems we had in place worked, and they always would, so long as I didn't disrupt them too much.

Distracting myself with a hockey romance, I let the time slip by. It's only when one of the baristas comes and takes my cup away, asking if I'd like something else to drink, that I realize the time.

It's almost noon. Stephen and I have dinner plans tonight, a celebration of another manuscript complete. It'll be nothing special. A home cooked meal—courtesy of my lovely Stephen—and some wine. I like it that way. After all, it's not like I actually wrote a book. A tinge of guilt and sadness passes through me.

I thank the barista, grab my coat, and head for the door.

I can cry about it while driving home in my Range Rover.

FIVE

Stephen laughs through a mouthful of steak and potatoes, doing his best to hold back the tears. But me, I'm half doubled over the candlelit table, laughing so hard that I end up dropping my fork onto my plate.

We have both just admitted to each other our most embarrassing moment, and while mine is relatively basic —I'd gotten locked in a bathroom stall in school once—his is downright hilarious.

He'd been participating in his first mud run, and halfway through, had somehow shit himself. He hoped that nobody would notice, because after all, it was *mud*, but they ended up shutting down the event due to a now-unsanitary mud pit.

"I'm serious!" He finally says, having swallowed his food. "I wanted to die."

"Wait, wait, you said your friends drove you to the event, right?"

"Yeah."

"So ..."

"I know what you're thinking. I had to walk home."

I choke on another stream of laughter and when it subsides, I reach for my glass. "You're something else, Stephen."

He grunts. "That's why I have to use the bathroom every time before I leave the house now. The great mud run incident."

He forks another piece of steak into his mouth.

A smile worms its way across my face, all the tension and stress and guilt from this morning having faded away. It's times like these that I'm grateful for him.

"Thank you, Stephen. Honestly. This is just what I needed." I take another sip of wine, the warmth of it spreading through me, loosening the tight coil in my chest.

"You deserve nights like this," he says, his voice gentle as he presses his warm hand over mine. "You've been working too hard, locked away in your office all day. I don't know how you keep everything together."

I smile faintly, twirling the stem of my wine glass between my fingers. "You'd be surprised how often it feels like I'm barely holding it together."

"You make it all look so effortless."

Effortless. The word lands heavily in my chest, and before I can stop myself, the wine does what wine does—it loosens my tongue.

"It's not," I say, my voice soft, almost hesitant. "It's not effortless, Stephen. It's... complicated."

He leans forward. "Complicated how?"

I hesitate, the confession lingering on the edge of my tongue. A part of me screams to hold it back, but the wine makes it easier to ignore that voice. I take a deep breath.

"I... I have something called aphantasia," I say, the words slipping out faster than I expected.

Stephen blinks, his confusion evident. "Aphantasia?"

"It means I can't see things in my mind," I explain, swirling the wine in my glass as I search for the right words. "Like, if you close your eyes and try to picture an apple, you can probably see it, right? Red or green, shiny, sitting on a table or something. But for me, there's just... nothing. Just darkness."

He leans back slightly, processing this. "So... you can't picture anything? At all?"

I shake my head. "No. And it's not just images. I can't imagine faces, places, even scenes. Everything is just... words. Sounds. Feelings. But no pictures."

Stephen's brow furrows, his confusion deepening, but it doesn't register for me.

The words continue tumbling out. "When I was in school, I had this English teacher. Old fart named Mr. Thompson. He was the first to know, and he made fun of me in front of the whole class." I pause, before chuckling to myself in a low voice. "If only he could see me now."

Stephen opens his mouth to ask something, but just then, a sharp knock at the door cuts through the air, startling us both.

My hand freezes mid-air, gripping the wine glass tightly. My heart races. A small voice in the back of my mind whispers, *Nothing bad ever happens when the doorbell rings. It's only when someone knocks that you have something to worry about.*

The knock comes again, louder this time, almost violent in the way it shakes the door. The sound jolts me back to the present, and I realize how much I'd been talking—how dangerously close to the truth I'd come.

What if Stephen realized that I wasn't actually writing my books? What would he think of me then?

Standing abruptly, I tell Stephen, "Stay here."

He calls after me, "Wait, were you expecting someone?"

"No," I call back, my voice tight.

The sound of my heels clicking against the hardwood floor echoes in the quiet house as I make my way to the door. The knock sounds a third time, even harsher now, and I hesitate, my hand hovering over the doorknob.

Through the stained glass, I can see a silhouette standing on the doorstep. There's something clutched in her hand, but I can't make out what it is. And it seems that she's seen my silhouette as well, because she stops knocking.

Instead, she stares at me through the glass, murky and disfigured. I swallow, the hairs standing up along the back of my neck. After a deep breath, I don the face of Miss Murder and pull the door open.

My eyes run over the older woman, taking in her disheveled appearance. The buttons of her heavy sweater are misaligned, and it looks like her hair hasn't been washed in weeks.

My gaze drifts downward, and I realize that she's clutching my latest bestseller, *Don't Breathe Twice*—the very same book I was on the talk show about.

I breathe a sigh of relief. A fan. She must have seen

me on Alyssa Lake's show and come for an autograph. I'm a little disturbed by the fact that the woman knows where I live, but I suppose that's the world these days. Information is just too readily available for those who seek it. It would probably be smart to start thinking about security or a gated entrance to my drive. I make a small note of it, before forcing a polite smile.

"Hi, can I help you?" I ask.

To my surprise, the fan steps forward, letting the light from inside the house spill over her face. My smile falters as I see the rage in her bloodshot eyes and her twisted snarl.

"You can tell me how you knew." The woman's voice trembles.

"I'm sorry? Knew what?"

The woman thrusts the book at me and I stumble back a step. The book's opened to a page, and it's filled with colored sticky notes. In fact, the entire book seems to be.

I glance up at her, confused.

"My son," the woman says, her voice breaking.

"I'm not sure I'm understanding what you're saying."

The woman snatches the book from my hand, before pulling a folded piece of paper from her pocket. Her breathing is heavy, and with shaking hands, she tries to unfold the paper.

My heart starts to pound, afraid to see what's on the paper.

"Listen, I'm in the middle of dinner with my boyfriend. Perhaps it would be best to do this later when—"

She shoves the still-folded paper into my hands. A moment later, I see what it is.

A police report.

"You wrote about his death. Every detail, down to the position he was found in, the exact way he died. These aren't things you could've made up. They weren't available to the public."

My blood runs cold as I scan the paper. Words blur together: asphyxiation, alleyway, black cord. I try to picture the scene, but, as always, my imagination goes dark—no images form.

"I... I didn't..."

"You didn't what? Write this?" the woman snaps, jabbing a finger at the book. "Your name's on the cover. You've been profiting off his death, *Miss Murder!*"

"I... I didn't know," I stammer, my voice weak and shaking. The words sound hollow even to me. "There must be some kind of mistake."

The woman steps forward, her finger jabbing painfully into my chest. "A mistake?" she spits. Raising her voice even louder, she asks, "How do you explain knowing things that were never released to the public?"

"I don't... I didn't..." My hands tremble, clutching the police report she shoved into them like a weapon. My mind is a blur of denial and panic, grasping for a way to make this stop.

"Don't lie to me!" she screams, her voice cracking with grief. Tears spill down her face, but they do nothing to soften the fury in her bloodshot eyes. "How do you know these things about my son? Who'd you pay to get this information? What kind of monster are you?"

The walls of the room seem to close in around me. I take an instinctive step back, bumping into the edge of the console table by the door. My hand fumbles for something solid—anything I can hold onto—because I feel like I'm falling, spiraling into the dark.

The woman steps closer. "You'll pay for this," she hisses through clenched teeth. "The whole world will know what you've done."

A sudden sound—footsteps, steady and deliberate—cuts through the chaos.

"Luna? What's going on?"

Stephen's voice, calm but laced with concern, slices through the tension. He steps into the hallway, his brows furrowed as he takes in the scene.

The woman's head snaps toward him, her body stiffening as she evaluates the new presence. For a moment, the three of us are frozen, locked in the tension.

Then, from the back of the house, a faint beep breaks the silence. The rhythmic hum of a machine follows—the sound of my mother's equipment monitoring her vitals.

The woman's eyes flick toward the sound, her anger faltering for a split second. Recognition flashes across her face, mingling with confusion and something softer—doubt, maybe.

Her gaze shifts back to me, darting between my face and the hallway where the sound came from. The rage in her eyes dims just slightly, replaced by a flicker of hesitation.

"You can't hide this forever," she says, her voice lower now. She takes a step back, clutching the book tightly to her chest, and points at me. "People will know."

Before I can respond, she turns on her heel and storms out, the door swinging shut behind her with a force that rattles the frame.

For a moment, the house is silent except for the faint hum of my mother's machines. Then I notice the police report lying on the floor where she dropped it.

Stephen moves closer, his face lined with worry. "Who was that?" he asks, his voice careful.

I don't answer immediately. My hands tremble as I pick up the police report, again scanning the details: asphyxiation, alleyway, black cord. The words blur together as the weight of her accusation sinks in.

Stephen touches my arm gently. "Luna?"

My mind races, piecing together fragments of thoughts that refuse to form a coherent picture. Has my ghostwriter been using police reports as inspiration for these novels? That might explain how they were able to send these perfect, haunting manuscripts *every* month. But how would they have access to this kind of information?

A shaky breath escapes me, and strangely, a laugh bubbles out of me. I don't know if it's the wine or how heightened the tension had been, but my laughter rises until I'm laughing as nearly as hard as I had been at the dinner table.

"Luna," Stephen says again. He presses his hand against my back. "What's going on?"

I glance at him, shaking my head as the laughter finally subsides.

"I don't know," I whisper, suddenly feeling like an empty shell, void of all the wine's warmth. Fear grips my heart, squeezing even tighter when I hear more of the beeps and drones coming from my mother's room.

My mother is only alive because of my success, and I know that it's things like these that destroy authors' careers. What if Alyssa Lake found out about this woman's dark accusation? I would be *done* for.

Stephen pulls me into a hug, and wrapped in his arms, I hope that this will all just go away. I tell myself that Miss Murder is too large to be taken down so easily by what must be a simple, unfortunate coincidence. After all, it's not like there's only ever been *one* man murdered in an alleyway with a black cord.

But deep down, some part of me knows that this is just the beginning.

SIX

My memory of that evening is a little murky. I know Stephen and I returned to dinner, and that I made the poor choice to pour myself another glass of wine, hoping to drown the lingering thoughts from the woman's accusations. It didn't work.

The wine dulled the edges of my fear for a while, but when I woke the next morning with a pounding migraine, the thoughts came roaring back. I wondered when I'd see cops standing on my doorstep, and when the headlines would spill across the internet, dismantling the carefully constructed persona of Miss Murder. They would probably read something like *Bestselling Author Profits from Real-Life Tragedy*.

The inevitable would happen. The money would dry up. The ability to afford my mother's care would collapse, and she wouldn't survive.

But none of that happened.

A week passed, and armageddon never came. The

woman hadn't returned, the police didn't knock, and my world hadn't fallen apart.

I sit in my leather chair, swiveling gently from side to side, my eyes stuck on the police report sitting on my desk. Its edges are slightly curled now from where I've handled it too much, reading and rereading the details. Each time, I tell myself the same thing: It must have been an isolated, grief-driven outburst.

Because the alternative is unthinkable.

With a heavy sigh, I push the report aside and return to my laptop, losing myself in the mindless routine of replying to emails, finalizing the cover for *The Broken Boy*, and planning my next Momnt livestream. The motions are mechanical, numbing in a way I desperately need.

When I finally close my laptop, the evening light spills golden across my floor-to-ceiling windows. The horizon is painted in soft pinks and oranges, and for a blessed moment, my mind is silent.

Until my phone buzzes.

The Momnt notification is routine—I get tagged all the time. Fans love sharing glowing reviews, and occasionally I'll respond, setting off a flurry of excitement among my followers. I swipe to open it without thinking.

But it's not that.

It's something far worse.

My heart skips as the livestream opens, and the woman's face fills the screen. She looks more put together now, with makeup carefully applied and her hair neatly combed. But her expression is no less intense, no less full of purpose.

"My name is Val Felder. My son's name was Cody Felder, and Miss Murder profited off his death," the woman says, holding up *Don't Breathe Twice*. The familiar cover in her hands looks warped, misshapen, like it doesn't belong. "Details in this story—specific, personal things—were never in the public police report. So how could she have known?"

My throat tightens, and I glance at the live viewer count. It's modest, but climbing steadily. Most of the comments seem skeptical, fans rushing to my defense, calling the woman crazy.

But she doesn't falter. Her eyes flick down to read the comments, and though she looks shaken for a moment, she steels herself and presses on.

She starts listing facts.

One by one, she lays them out: the way her son was found, the exact position of his body, the method of his death. Her voice trembles as she connects them with passages from my book. The longer she speaks, the more convincing her argument becomes. Some viewers begin to waver, their comments reflecting growing horror.

I can't watch anymore. I close the app, my stomach twisting.

It's only a few people now, but that's all it takes. A single snowflake to start the avalanche.

I lean over my desk, digging my fingers into my scalp to stop the storm of thoughts barreling through my mind. *Am I making money off bloodshed?* And *how did the ghostwriter know all of this stuff?*

A sharp knock at the door jolts me, and I jump.

"Ms. Harrow?"

It's Vincent's voice, steady but firm.

"Yes?" I answer, pressing a hand to my chest, willing my racing heart to calm.

"Can I speak with you for a moment?"

I exhale sharply, trying to gather myself. Running a hand through my hair, I stand and open the door. Vincent stands there, his expression anxious, his posture tense.

"Would you come with me, please?" he says, his voice unusually clipped.

My brows furrow. "Is everything okay?"

He doesn't answer.

Instead, he turns and starts walking down the hall toward my mother's room.

A knot of unease forms in my stomach, and I realize with growing certainty that whatever Vincent wants to show me has nothing to do with the woman—or her accusations. But it might be worse.

The hallway to my mother's room feels longer than usual, and Vincent's silence only amplifies the growing weight in my chest.

He opens the door, and I step quietly inside. The soft, sterile light washes over the familiar sight of my mother, still and frail in her bed, her features relaxed in a way that could almost be peaceful. But something feels off, and I can't quite place it.

In a hushed voice to keep from waking her, I ask him, "What's wrong?"

Vincent moves to the monitors, pointing to the screen. "Her blood pressure has been erratic. Small fluctuations at first, but they've become more pronounced over the last two days." He hesitates, his fingers brushing the edge of her chart. "She's been showing signs of discomfort."

"Discomfort?" The word catches in my throat. "How can she feel anything? She—" My gaze shifts to my mother, her eyelids fluttering ever so slightly, the only movement in her otherwise unresponsive body.

Vincent nods, his tone clinical but soft. "Even with locked-in syndrome, it's possible for patients to experience pain or muscle spasms. It's subtle, but it's there. Her reactions to touch have been different—tension in her facial muscles, slight shifts in her breathing patterns."

My hands clench at my sides as I absorb his words. "So, what does this mean? Is she... suffering?"

"I can't say for certain," he admits, his voice gentle. "But I believe she may be. I wanted to inform you before making any adjustments to her care. I think we should increase her pain management regimen."

"Pain management?" The words feel foreign, like they don't belong in this room, in this context. "You're saying she needs more medication?"

He nods, glancing at the monitors again. "Just a small adjustment. It should help alleviate any discomfort and stabilize her vitals."

I take a shaky step closer to the bed, my gaze fixed on her face. Her expression is serene, but now I can't unsee the faint flicker of strain in the corner of her mouth, or the barely perceptible twitch of her fingers.

This, on top of the grieving woman's livestream happening *right now,* makes it suddenly feel like the room is closing in on me, the air too thick to breathe.

"How come you didn't let me know when it started happening?"

"These things sometime resolve themselves on their own. But unfortunately, this time it hasn't." He can see how stressed out I am, and in a guilt-tinged voice, he adds, "I should've told you sooner. I didn't want to worry you unnecessarily."

Unnecessarily. The word hangs in the air, hollow and meaningless. Worry feels like the only thing I'll ever know anymore.

I sink into the chair beside her bed, reaching for her hand. It's cool to the touch, her fingers limp in my grasp. The rows of my novels lining the shelves catch my eye, their glossy covers a sharp contrast to the fragile reality in front of me. This is why I do it, I remind myself. This is why I need the money, why I need the books to sell, why I need the manuscripts to keep coming.

But for the first time, the mantra feels hollow.

"I'll make the changes carefully," Vincent says, his voice pulling me back to the present. "I'll monitor her closely. If there's any issues, we can reassess."

I nod, though I barely register his words. My eyes are locked on her face, searching for something—anything—that will tell me I'm doing the right thing. That I haven't built this fragile, precarious life on a foundation of lies and blood.

"I'll give you a moment," Vincent says softly, stepping toward the door. "Let me know if you need anything."

When the door clicks shut behind him, the silence is deafening. I lean closer to my mother, brushing a strand of hair from her forehead. My eyes drift back to the novels and I can't help but wonder: what would my mother think if she knew that these stories might be fueling something sinister?

"I'm sorry," I whisper, my voice cracking, hating my dependence on these damned manuscripts.

I stay there long enough for me to fall asleep in the chair next to my mother. I wish I could say that I slept peacefully, having escaped into a dark space free from all the nightmares. But truth is, the nightmares chased me into my sleep, their claws raking against my consciousness in a way that leaves scars.

It's only when Stephen wakes me with a gentle kiss on the head that I wake, no more free from the haunting thought than before.

He sees the look on my face and frowns. "Is everything okay?"

I start to nod and lie that I'm fine, but I hesitate. And slowly, I shake my head, tears filling my eyes. He wraps his arms around me, surrounding me in his warmth.

"Is this because of your mother?" he whispers, taking care not to wake her up. "Vincent told me everything."

My voice chokes as I try to answer, and he takes my hand, leading me out of the room and to the kitchen. He passes me a drink of water and makes me a buttered bagel, before resting back against the counter.

Again, I'm reminded of how lucky I am to have him. He knows I haven't eaten or drank in hours. He's here to take care of me in all the ways I need.

With a deep, shuddering breath, I finally speak. "Do you remember that fan?"

"From a week ago?"

I nod.

"How could I forget?"

"She thinks that one of my books is connected to her son's murder."

"What?" He blinks. "That's ridiculous."

I can't help but think, *Is it?*

"I get that your books are crazy detailed. But everyone knows that's your magic. You make things feel real."

He's trying to comfort me, but the words sting, because I know that's *not* my magic. They're *not* my words.

I drink from my glass of water and take a bite of the bagel.

"Is that all you're concerned about?" He offers me a smile. "I wouldn't worry, Luna. This'll pass."

"I thought so, but she's gone onto Momnt. She's telling everyone."

He pauses, a hint of doubt flickering across his face. "Are they believing her?"

"Some, maybe. Not everyone."

He breathes a sigh of relief, and his smile returns. "Then you have nothing to worry about. Look, you were just on the Alyssa Lake Show. There's going to be haters. There's going to be people jealous of your success, and they'll do anything they can to tear you down. You've got to ignore it, okay? Everything's going to be fine. I promise you."

I set aside my bagel and water and step into his arms again. I breathe him in, letting the scent of his cologne put me at ease.

"If there's anything I can do for you, you let me know, okay? I mean it. I would do *anything* for you."

"I know," I whisper, my voice barely audible against his chest. I really don't know what I would do without him.

"That's my girl," he says, brushing a strand of hair from my face. "Now, eat your bagel. No more spiraling. I'll see you in bed, okay?"

His footsteps pad out of the kitchen and I take a seat at the kitchen counter, taking another bite out of the bagel.

Despite everything, it turns to sand in my mouth. I swallow mechanically, trying to ground myself. Maybe Stephen is right. Maybe this will all blow over.

It would be best to go to bed, try and get some actual rest. But I'm a little afraid of what will happen when I close my eyes. I decide to return to the office, and passing by the bedroom, I let Stephen know that I have a few things to wrap up.

He tries hard to hide the disappointment in his eyes, but I see it, and I ignore it anyway, knowing that there's nothing I can do about it. This was our reality, sometimes. I'm a bit of a workaholic. If I can't write the book, I can damn well do everything else.

I step into my office, the leather chair groaning softly as I sink into it. The air here presses against me, thick with the scent of typewritten ink. Before, I'd always found it welcoming. But now, it feels alien and toxic.

My eyes drift to the police report, still perched on the corner of my desk, its edges curling under my gaze. I've tried ignoring it. Tried pretending it doesn't exist. But the words are still there, waiting.

I reach for *Don't Breathe Twice*, the cover slick under my trembling fingers. It's heavier than I remember. Slowly, I open it, flipping to the chapter I know she mentioned. My stomach twists as I read it. I reach the part the killer lifts the black cord, looping it around the victim's neck. He counts the minutes as the man struggles, and when he's finished, he etches the number of minutes into the black cord with sadistic pleasure.

A cold chill passes over me.

I check the police report. It's not noted there, but there is a picture of the murder weapon, the black cord they'd found disposed of in another alley over a mile away. I pull it close, and though the picture is grainy, I think I see four distinct scratches in the cord.

The glass of water on my desk quivers as my hand trembles. My pulse roars in my ears. The room feels darker now, shadows creeping across the shelves lined with my books. I can't breathe, can't think as I stare at them, because I'm held prisoner by a single, horrifying thought.

What if *all* my books are based on real murders?

SEVEN

The thought won't let me go.

Even after I set the book and police report aside, pushing them to the farthest corner of my desk, the idea clings to me like smoke. What if all my books are based on real murders? The question loops in my mind, louder and sharper with every pass.

I grip the edge of the desk, fingers digging into the wood as if that might ground me, tethering me to some version of reality where this isn't true.

My gaze shifts to the shelves again, the glossy spines gleaming under the dim glow of the desk lamp. There's a strange weight to them now, like each book is holding a secret I was never meant to uncover.

My stomach churns as I reach for another title—*Whisper No More*. It was my third book, and one of Stephen's favorites. My hands tremble as I pull it free and flip to the scene that always unsettled me when I read it back then—the murder in the library. I swallow hard and grab my laptop.

Small steps, I tell myself. Just... check.

The screen glows to life, and my hands hover over the keyboard, hesitant. What exactly am I even looking for? What do I type? After a moment, I start with something simple: the book's title and the words *library* and *murder*.

Nothing. Just a few pages across the internet raving about my book.

Biting my lip, I try again, this time leaving out the title.

Still, nothing.

I search the internet repeatedly, trying different variations of words, anything that came to mind. And just as I'm starting to feel a glimmer of hope that perhaps this incident could be isolated to *Don't Breathe Twice*, I find it.

The headline cuts through me like a knife.

Unsolved Murder in Whitmore Baffles Investigators.

I click into the article, and my vision blurs as I skim the details. Just like the book, there was a young woman who'd been strangled with her own scarf. She'd been found deep in the dusty archives a day later. No witnesses, no suspects, no answers.

I read the scene in the book again. While there were no distinguishing details that could be used to identify the link between the two like in *Don't Breathe Twice*, it was still close enough that it made my throat tighten.

Another book. I have to know if this is just coincidence stacked upon coincidence. I check another book, *Shallow Graves*, and the result is the same. Headlines. Real people. Real deaths.

It's only when I hear a soft knock at the door that I

realize the morning light has begun to spill through the windows. A sudden wave of exhaustion passes through me, and it has little to do with the lack of sleep.

"Yeah," I call out.

The door cracks open, Stephen's face peering through. He frowns, surprised by the sight of my office floor cluttered with all the books I've ever released. His worried eyes drift to me.

"Everything okay?"

"Fine," I say in a sharp, clipped tone. I put on my best fake smile I can. "Why?"

He frowns, but he doesn't pursue it. Hopefully, he doesn't think I'm drowning in the realization that my books must be based on real murders, and thinks that I'm stressed about a deadline or something like that.

His eyes flit back to the books on the ground, and full pause later, he asks, "Would you like breakfast?"

"What?"

"Breakfast, Luna. I'm guessing you haven't eaten, have you?"

I haven't. Food is the last thing on my mind right now. I shake my head, and a second later, I hear the door click shut. With a heavy groan, I lay flat on the floor, staring up at the ceiling. I wait for an answer to come to me. There *must* be one.

But next thing I know, I'm asleep.

I jolt awake, as though my body suddenly remembered

that there was a life or death situation going on. Maybe that's a bit dramatic, but in a way, that's what it *was*.

If readers began to realize that Miss Murder was writing her books on the details of *real* murders, then everything I'd done these last two years would evaporate within the blink of an eye. The money, the notoriety, my mother's care—it would all disappear.

My body groans as I get to my feet, aches and pains shooting through my back. I stare down at the books scattered across the floor, contemplating whether I should clean them up. Clean space, clean mind, right?

The idea is laughable. How would cleaning my office help me with what I was facing? The sharp *ding* of a notification pulls my attention to my phone, resting on the desk with low battery.

It's Momnt again.

I hold my breath as I open the app, breathing a sigh of relief when I see that the notification is just a reminder of my planned livestream coming up.

Settling into the warmth of my leather chair, I take a moment away from my brain and scroll through my feed. A trending hashtag is suggested in the search bar at the top.

#MissMurder

For a moment, fear strikes at me, worry creeping along the back of my neck at the idea that perhaps readers had *already* begun to realize the dark details behind my stories.

But then I take a deep breath. This wasn't exactly uncommon. On more than half of my releases, #Miss-

Murder ended up reaching top ten trending status across Momnt. Some for more than a week straight.

With my appearance on the Alyssa Lake Show, I imagine that might have been enough to create another resurgence in popularity despite the fact that my next release is in two week's time. Alyssa had that effect on authors with how large her platform was.

I follow the trending hashtag, expecting to find shared thoughts on the details leaked through the talk-show, or clips of readers getting their books signed by me.

But instead, I find clips of the grieving woman's video tagged to me. My heart skips a beat as I watch through several videos, hearing how some readers are finding "weird" that my book matches her police report so carefully. Speculation is starting to pick up.

Then, I notice the second trending hashtag, posted at the bottom of several posts.

#LunaHarrow

A curse slips between my teeth as I bend over my phone, trying to dig into the storm to see just how bad it is. But before I can, my phone dies.

I toss the phone onto the desk with more force than intended, the sound startlingly loud in the quiet. The room feels unnaturally still as I sit there, staring at the lifeless phone. My hands rest limply in my lap, useless. I could get up, grab the charger, plug the damn thing in, and face whatever chaos is waiting for me.

But I don't.

The thought of seeing more clips, more accusations, more people connecting dots I didn't even realize existed until a few hours ago—it makes my chest feel like it's caving in. If I plug my phone in, if I open that app again, it makes all of this real.

And I'm not ready for that.

I glance at the books scattered around me, their glossy covers glinting faintly in the dim light. These were supposed to be my triumphs. But now? Now, they feel like time bombs. Each book a ticking reminder of the lies I've built my empire on.

My insides roil, a sickly wave rolling over me as I think back to the grieving woman's accusations. The thing is, I didn't know. I didn't know about her son or the others. But I should have asked. I should have looked harder, questioned the perfection of every manuscript that landed neatly on my desk. Instead, I ignored the gnawing discomfort, content to keep my head down and let the words come.

A coward and a fraud. That's what I am.

I push back from my desk and stand, my legs stiff from sitting too long. The room feels too small, too claustrophobic. I need air. Or maybe just distance.

As I step outdoors, my bare feet touching the soft grass of the lawn, a thought makes its way into my head.

I need to get ahead of this. I need to do *something*.

But how? Do I go public with the truth? Or do I try to discredit Val before she gains even *more* traction?

Neither of those options feel right, but I can't do nothing. Doing nothing is the same as signing my own death certificate at this point, or rather, my mother's.

I try to clear my mind, breathe in the fresh air and for a moment, just a moment, appreciate the beauty around me. I close my eyes and take in the peace, let it seep into me and calm my anxiety and my worries and my racing heart.

When I open them next, I know what I need to do. There's only one thing readers want, and I can give it to them.

Heading back indoors, I head straight for my office, grabbing my charger on the way. My boyfriend calls after me, but I ignore him, shutting the door after me.

Plugging in the phone, it buzzes immediately. Notifications begin to flood in. Messages, emails, tags from comments and posts—it's endless. One notification stands out, a fresh video from Val.

My jaw clenches as her face fills the screen.

"I won't stop until the truth comes out. Luna Harrow knows something about my son's death, and I'm going to prove it. Watch out, Miss *Murder*. I'm coming for you."

The video stops there. I look into her eyes on the screen. Grief lingers there, but so does something else. Something deeper, darker, and it's aimed straight at me.

I swipe away from the video and open up my messages. I have a plan, but first there's something I desperately need to know.

Did you write all of these books on details from police reports?

A thought pops into my head. All this time, I'd been focused on myself, not once thinking about the fact that there's a second person behind the persona of Miss Murder. Whoever they are, they must have seen the trending hashtags about me. Why haven't they said anything?

Maybe they're not worried.

But me messaging them, showing them how spooked I am... would that be enough to make them think twice about the deal we'd struck? My eyes widen as I realize that just by confronting the ghostwriter, I could be risking everything.

I delete the message. I have a plan anyways. There was no point in digging myself into a deeper hole than the one I was already in.

I close out the Momnt app and text Janice.

Hey Janice, have you finished with any edits? I need to release 'The Broken Boy' sooner than planned.

Two minutes later, I get a response.

Just finished the first pass.

I smile and type back, *Can we meet today? A first pass might be fine.*

My message was read right away, but it was a few minutes before she responded.

If that's what you want. We can meet in the usual place. 2:00?

Perfect. See you then.

I put my phone aside and with my hands over my head, finally draw a deep breath of relief. This'll all go away soon, because I know one thing that Val does not. I know what readers want more than anything else.

The next book.

As soon as they have it in their hands, this'll all disappear. Everybody will get sucked into the newest story and excitement, and they'll forget all about her, her son, and the unfortunate coincidence his death has with my book. At least, that's what I tell myself when I head for the bedroom in an attempt to get more rest before meeting Janice.

But rest doesn't come. Nightmares do.

EIGHT

The exchange with Janice goes as planned. She shows up at precisely two, wearing the same dress but in a different neutral shade, with a green ribbon in place of blue.

Just like last time, though, I noticed that she was strangely tense. Maybe it was something to do with the break in routine, with requesting the edited manuscript earlier than normal. I know she preferred to do multiple passes through the book to double check her work. But if she had a problem with it, she didn't make it known as she passed over the manuscript and a digitally written copy of it.

And other than a few grammatical errors that she corrected, the book was ready to go. I passed her a check, with an added bonus on top for the quick turnaround time.

By the time I made it home, the cover was ready too. Normally, my cover artist wasn't available for same day turnaround. But his tune changed after I tripled his fee.

And while his cover wasn't his best work, it was acceptable enough to do the job.

The book was ready for publishing.

Now, I sat in front of my phone with a full face of makeup on, the powerful picture of Miss Murder staring back at me with a radiant smile in red lipstick. I owned these readers. Not Val Felder.

I press record.

The camera captures me perfectly. I lean forward slightly, my smile warm but commanding. "Hello, my beautiful fans. You probably didn't expect to hear from me this early, especially since it's not the first of the month yet. But I have a bit of a surprise, on the back of the Alyssa Lake Show."

I pause, letting the moment build. Then my smile widens and I let a little scream of excitement. "I'm releasing my next book today! *The Broken Boy* will go live at midnight, available to download everywhere. As for paperbacks, hardback, and audiobooks, those will be available over the next week or two."

I still had to figure those out.

"I know it's not the first of the month like usual, and I promise I'll explain later. But for now, I couldn't wait any longer to share this story with you. This one's special."

I pause, leaning forward conspiratorially, like I'm sharing a secret with a trusted friend. "Let's just say, this book came to me when I needed it most. And I think, after everything, you'll feel the same way too."

I hit stop.

Reviewing the clip, I nod in satisfaction. It's the perfect blend of genuine and enigmatic, a carefully curated version of myself that has kept readers hooked since the day I published that first manuscript.

The upload begins, and I type out the caption: *Sometimes, a story can't wait. 'The Broken Boy' is here—available now. Link in bio.*

I post it, and almost instantly, the reactions begin to pour in. At first, it's a flood of excitement and love:

A surprise drop? YES! Miss Murder delivers AGAIN!

I just grabbed it—let's gooooo!

Luna, you always know how to spoil us. I'm so ready for this one!

A genuine smile spreads across my face and I sit back in my chair, breathing a deep sigh of relief as the weight disappeared from my shoulders. I could feel the tide shifting back my way, and knew that soon, Val Felder and all of the problems she brought my way would be nothing but a distant memory. I could go back to worrying only about my deepest insecurities of being unable to write, and stop fearing the reality of having everything taken from me.

My stomach rumbles and I realize that I can't remember the last time I had a decent meal. All throughout my late lunch, I keep an eye on my phone. The plan continues to work. The response from the fans is still positive.

But then I see a comment come in.

"*A surprise drop? Or a distraction?*"

"*@ValFelder, what do you think?*"

"*Hey @MissMurder, is this based on another murder?*"

My chest tightens as the notifications roll in faster,

the thread already becoming a battlefield of speculation and doubt. And then, a new post from Val appears in the tagged mentions.

My sandwich sits uneasy in my belly. I hesitate before clicking.

Her stitched video is slick and brutal, starting with a clip from my post. "This book came to me when I needed it most," I say in the video, my radiant smile frozen in place. Then, Val's voice cuts in: "Oh, I'll bet it did, Luna. Let's talk about why."

The screen shifts to her, holding my book in one hand and the police report in the other. Her expression is tight, her words sharp. "Here's what's raw and honest: losing someone you love and seeing their death fictionalized for profit."

She flips to a marked page in the book, reading a passage aloud. The vivid description of a body found in an alley matches the report down to the smallest detail. I scroll through the comments on her video, and they are getting progressively worse.

I stare blankly at the wall as my pulse races. My carefully calculated surprise release is already slipping from my control, dragged under by the weight of Val's accusations.

My hand shakes as I swipe away from the video. I see post after post start to roll in, each tagging me, each equally accusatory. Surprisingly, it's not fear that comes to the forefront of my mind, but shame.

You'll never write anything real.

I dig my fingers into my hair, each new post clawing at the guilt and fear I'd buried beneath the success—guilt of not having truly written my own book, and fear that I never would. I cling to the hope that *somehow*, this'll all stop. How many celebrities escaped controversy? When you add it up, versus the ones that have been canceled, it stands to reason that my odds seem pretty good. Right?

But then a new hashtag is suggested.

#LunaHarrowExposed

Shit.

NINE

Stephen sits across the outdoor table from me, munching on his burger with emphatic moans, completely oblivious of the storm that's headed our way. Somehow, he convinced me that I'd spent too long cooped up in my office, and that a breath of fresh air would do me some good.

I won't lie, the chill air does feel nice. Back there, trapped in the tight walls of my office and buried beneath the weight of endless notifications, I was starting to feel like I was stuck in hell.

Don't get me wrong, I *still* feel like I'm stuck in hell. But at least the cool air feels nice against my face.

"You're not going to eat?" Stephen asks past a mouthful of food. I glance up at him, suddenly wishing he would do me a favor and just shut up. Or at the very least, chew and swallow his food before speaking.

I shake my head, lowering my gaze back down to my phone. I chew on my fingernails as I stare at an unsent draft, sitting in my messages.

It's addressed to Val.

Her name glows at the top of the screen, and I reread the draft for what feels like the hundredth time.

How much would it cost to feel at peace?

I want to send it, just to have something—anything—that feels like action. But my thumb hovers over the send button, and a sick feeling coils in my stomach. What am I even asking? How do you put a price on closure when I'm part of the reason she doesn't have any? She'd never forgive me. And worse, she might screenshot it and share it with the online world. Most likely, she *would*.

My phone buzzes in my hand, making me jump. It's Stephen. I glance up to see him still staring at me, his burger gone along with all his fries. His eyebrows are drawn in frustration.

"Luna, you've been staring at that thing for the last fifteen minutes. What's so important?"

I quickly lock the screen and shove the phone into my bag. "Work," I say, too quickly. "Just trying to catch up on emails."

"Right," he says, dragging the word out like it's a knife across stone. "Because what you really needed to do today was sit in another chair and stare at another screen."

His words land heavier than I expect, cutting through the thin barrier I've been using to keep myself together. "You're the one who dragged me out here," I snap. "I told you I had a lot on my plate."

Stephen sets his burger down with deliberate slowness, brushing his hands against his napkin. His gaze locks onto mine. "What's on your plate, Luna? Besides ignoring me and spiraling into whatever's going on in that head of yours?"

"Don't," I say, warning him off with a raised hand. "Don't act like you don't know what I'm dealing with right now."

His brow rises and he scoffs, "Are you serious right now?"

The soft breeze stills, and his raised voice is loud enough to draw a glance from the couple sitting at the next table. But he doesn't care.

"I've been patient, but it's like you're not even here anymore."

I open my mouth, ready to tell him he's wrong, but the words die on my tongue. What could I even say? That I'm terrified everything that I've worked for is about to collapse in on me? That the secret I've hidden from the world, from *him*, is leading me to be complicit in profiting off other murders?

I know I could open up to him. He'd listen to me, take me in and reassure me. But he couldn't make everything alright, and for that reason alone, I find myself saying the only words that might help.

"I'm sorry."

Stephen studies me for a long moment, his expression softening slightly, though the tension in his jaw remains. At last, he says, "Okay."

Then my phone buzzes. Another notification.

He draws a sharp breath, stands, and tosses a few bills on the table. "I'll see you at home."

"Wait!" I call after him as he walks away, leaving me alone with the chill air biting harder than before.

"Stephen!"

He ignores me as he gets into the car and drives off. It takes me a minute to realize that he was my ride home. It's not an impossibly long walk, but it will take me at least twenty minutes if I started off now.

I stare at the place we'd parked, and my heart kind of falls. He had never done that before, leaving me stranded without an easy way home.

The couple nearby is staring at me, pity in their eyes.

"Learn to mind your own business!" I shout, making them jump. Before they can say anything back, I'm up and out of my seat and headed home.

There were problems that needed fixing, and sitting at a local burger shack was not the place to do that. As I walk home, I open my phone and check the notification. #LunaHarrowExposed is now in the top three trending hashtags, with millions of views on the controversy spilling across the internet.

Video after video are tagging me, wondering why the normally attentive Miss Murder was suddenly avoidant. The fans are demanding a response, and the longer I went without one, the worse the fallout would be. It didn't take a publicist to know that.

With a frustrated sigh, I swipe over to my messages and delete the draft to Val. Sending her *anything* would be the death of me, I was sure of it.

Instead, I start drafting up a message that I could post. I go through multiple variations, and it's only when I'm two minutes from home that I come to a decent version that might be reassuring.

It has come to my attention the similarities between

Don't Breathe Twice and the unfortunate murder of an innocent. My deepest condolences go out to the innocent's mother, Val Felder. But to my fans, I must state that I would never profit from another's tragedy. My stories come from imagination and hard work.

I open the camera and start to record, but when I finish the video and stare into the eyes of Miss Murder, I can't help but think... she's guilt. *I'm* guilty. The stories come from imagination and hard work? That sounds defensive, stemming from a place of the deepest insecurity. Maybe that's because it *was*.

I shove my phone back into my bag, letting out a ragged breath as I reach the house. The walk has done little to clear my head. If anything, the cold has only made me even angrier.

When I push open the front door, I find Stephen sitting on the couch, his hands loosely clasped between his knees. He looks up at me, and the anger from earlier is gone, replaced by something else. Guilt. His lips part like he's about to say something, but I stomp past him without a word, not trusting myself to hear whatever apology he's trying to offer.

"Luna—" he starts, but I cut him off with the slam of my office door.

The familiar scent of typewritten ink and paper greets me. I drop into my chair, letting it envelop me as I rub my hands over my face, trying to push any thoughts of Stephen from my mind. He's right, of course. I haven't been present. But how can I be, when everything I'd built these last two years is starting to unravel.

I open my phone again and watch the recorded video

again. It's a bad idea. Every bone in my body is telling me that. I delete the video.

Instead, I switch to my messages. Charles Dickens. My mysterious ghostwriter and would-be benefactor, if not for the fact that they were using real life murders in the books they were gifting me.

For a long moment, I stare at the empty text box, fingers trembling over the keys. Finally, I type:

Have you seen what's happening?

A minute passes. Then two. Then five. Time drags by, until at long last, a little note beneath my message says *Read*. Three dots bounce for several seconds before Charles Dickens replies.

Yes.

I to want squeeze the life out of my phone. *Yes?* That's all they've got to say? My jaw clenches as I tap out a response.

So the details of one of your manuscripts is causing trouble.

I hover over the send button, suddenly aware that too sharp a tone could push them away. In which case, I had no more manuscripts coming my way, and the books that *were* published would bury me. I add onto the message.

I need help.

I hit send.

The response comes faster than I expected.

Stick to our routine. Don't question the process.

That's it. No acknowledgment of the brewing storm, no offer to fix it, no reassurance. Just the same cold efficiency that has carried this arrangement from the very start.

I lay my phone down on the desk and sit back, still staring at the screen. There's a familiarity about my Charles Dickens that's hard to put my finger on, but no matter how long I think on it, I can't come up with why.

With a heavy sigh, I put my phone to sleep and focus on administrative work. As much as I really don't want to do it, I know that there will be readers and fans—the ones who are either still supporting me or completely oblivious to the controversy—waiting on paperback, hardback, and audio versions of the book.

The paperback and hardback is relatively easy to sort out with a few back-and-forth emails with my cover design. Of course, I do prefer to have real copies in hand to check before putting them live, but I've done this over twenty times now, and if I'm honest, I can't bring myself to care too much right now.

The audio's sent my way late in the afternoon, an impressive herculean effort by my voice actors. I would expect nothing less after the insane fee I paid them for both their high quality work *and* a beyond fast turn-around time.

I download the file to my phone, shove my earbuds in, and start listening to the dark rendition of *The Broken Boy*. Listening to killer's perspective, I begin to walk around the house. Most people would make use of their time listening to audiobooks by cleaning or jogging on the treadmill. And normally I do. But there's a numbness about me that just has me walking through the halls, feet padding against the wooden flooring.

At one point, I glance out the window and see that it's raining. My Range Rover is the only car in the driveway, besides Vincent's Honda. Stephen must have left. With a shrug, I resume my mindless pacing of the house. A soft thud echoes behind me, and I spin around, noticing a hooded figure standing in the doorway.

The scream tears from my throat before I can stop it. My heart slams against my ribcage as I yank the earbuds out, the chilling voice of the audiobook disappearing into the tense silence. The figure in the doorway shifts, the hood falling back to reveal Vincent, his damp hair plastered to his forehead. His dark jacket is soaked through, rainwater dripping onto the floor in soft splashes.

"Ms. Harrow," he says in a calm voice, but I see him fighting the urge to smile. "I didn't mean to startle you."

I press a hand to my chest, trying to steady my breathing. "What the hell, Vincent? What are you doing sneaking around like that?"

His smile widens, the corners of his eyes crinkling. "I wasn't sneaking. It's raining out there. Thought I'd come in quietly and not track mud through your house."

I glance down at the pristine floor and the faint trail of water his shoes have left behind.

"Could've fooled me," I mutter, bending to grab a towel from a nearby cabinet. I toss it to him, and he catches it with ease, patting his hair dry. The sight of him, so casual and composed, starts to chip away at my lingering fear, leaving only embarrassment in its place.

"You alright?" he asks, his tone softening as he looks me over. His gaze lingers a moment too long, and I feel the heat of it prickling against my skin.

I nod quickly, crossing my arms over my chest. "Yeah. I'm fine. Just... wasn't expecting you."

He chuckles, low and warm, as he steps fully into the house. "Didn't mean to scare you like that. Guess that audiobook isn't helping much, huh?"

I glance down at the phone in my hand, reading the line of the paused track.

The killer moves closer, his shadow stretching over the boy.

I wince and close out the audiobook. "You're probably right."

The line hovers in my mind, and I shake it off. "Something like that."

Vincent gestures toward the hall. "How about we check on your mother? She's had a good day. Might help to see her."

A good day. Those words, rare as they are, are enough to soften the tension knotting my shoulders. I follow him down the hall, the sound of our footsteps blending with the faint patter of rain against the windows. When we reach her room, Vincent steps aside, allowing me to enter first.

The machines hum steadily alongside the faint beeping of the heart monitor. My mother's asleep, her face peaceful and full of color, her chest rising and falling with ease.

"She's been doing much better since we adjusted her medicine," Vincent whispers from behind me.

My mother's eyes flutter faintly, like she's aware someone's in the room. Maybe she's conscious. I step closer and brush a strand of hair from her forehead.

"Hi Mom," I whisper gently.

I find myself waiting for a response, but I know none

will come. I miss the old days, when she was healthy enough to at least crack a joke. In truth, I'd trade all of this money and fame just to have a few more of those days.

Vincent watches from the corner of the room. "You've got a lot on your plate, don't you?" he says softly.

I glance at him, surprised at how quickly he picked it up. I wonder what he's noticed. How much more I'm in my office these days? How much Stephen and I are struggling?

"Just... stressed about the release," I admit, the lie coming easily. "It's a lot to juggle."

He nods, his smile warm and reassuring. "You'll figure it out. You're smart like that." The way he says it, with such quiet conviction, makes something in me ache. It's a small moment, but his words settle over me like a blanket.

My gaze lingers on Vincent as he leaves the room, giving me time alone with my mother. A question gnaws at the edges of my thoughts: Where was Stephen right now? Why wasn't he the one reassuring me, offering quiet comfort instead of demanding more attention from me? Couldn't he see how hard everything is for me right now?

I stay by my mother's side a little longer, my fingers brushing lightly against hers as I spin stories—lies, really. I tell her how great the book release is going, how smoothly everything's falling into place. I talk about all the plans I have for the house, embellishing every detail as if those dreams weren't as empty as the silence in the room. She doesn't respond, but the steady rhythm of her breathing keeps me grounded.

When I finally run out of lies to tell, I slip my earbuds back in and press play on the audiobook. The killer's voice murmurs in my ears, low and dark, a strange kind of company. It's a little pathetic, I know, but I rest my head against her side, closing my eyes. Gently, I lift her hand and place it atop my head, pretending for a moment that she's stroking my hair the way she did when I was a child.

The killer's voice wraps around me like a lullaby, and soon, I'm fast asleep.

TEN

It's deep into the night when I wake. For a moment, I'm disoriented, unsure of where exactly I am. But the soft beeps and drones of my mother's equipment anchors me back to reality. I rub the sleep out of my eyes and realize that the audio track has stopped.

With a groan, I withdraw the earbuds from my ears and retreat from the room, shutting the door softly behind me to avoid waking my mother. That is, if I *could* wake her. While the doctors were entirely useless in helping me understand, I didn't want to accidentally wake her and leave her trapped in helpless consciousness for hours before she could fall back into the bliss of sleep.

I head down the hall and pause at the bedroom door. It's ajar, with soft snores drifting through the crack. Stephen must have come back pretty late. He only ever snores when he's exhausted. Hopefully he doesn't think I was stuck in my office, doing more work and ignoring him.

Sadness touches my heart. Perhaps I have been difficult, paying more attention to myself than to him. I mean, I know that it was for good reason, but still, he loves me and wants to be around me. Is that so bad?

I'll talk things over with him in the morning. Let him know what's been stressing me out. I wouldn't go so far as to confess my deeper guilt and struggles, but I'd let him know just how bad everything was getting. After all, I didn't expect him to know, with him not having much of a social media presence. Hopefully that would make him more sympathetic to my problems.

I gently push the door open, wincing as the hinges creak. I slip out of my clothing and change into my pajamas—oversized basketball shorts with an even larger oversized shirt. Stephen asked me once why I wear men's clothing to sleep, but I don't think he could ever understand how comfortable it is. Certainly not at his tall height.

Just before I'm about to get into bed, I realize how thirsty I am and carefully tip toe my way out of the room and down to the kitchen. I drink from a large glass, and as I set the glass back on the counter, something catches my eye near the door. Stephen's bag is slouched against the wall, half-open, with papers poking out at odd angles. That, in itself, isn't unusual—Stephen has a habit of leaving things just like this, like bags are meant to be bursting with their contents spilling over. But what is unusual is the corner of a familiar brown envelope poking out from the bag.

I glance back toward the stairs, the faint sound of Stephen's snores still drifting down from the bedroom. Slowly, carefully, I go to pull the envelope free.

My breath hitches.

It's heavier than usual, but it's *that* envelope. The same smooth, unassuming packaging that has arrived at my door every month for the last two years, always on the first of the month, like clockwork. It even has my name written clearly on the front. But this one... this one isn't supposed to be here yet. There's two weeks to go until it's supposed to arrive.

My fingers tremble as I hold the package. Hoping that it's all some sort of dark coincidence, I grab a knife and slice open the sealed flap.

The smell of typewritten ink wafts out.

I draw a deep, shuddering breath and reach into the envelope, withdrawing a stack of pages. I flip to the first page.

The descriptions leap out at me immediately, just as flawless and gripping as the day I'd first seen one of my ghostwriter's manuscripts.

A man stands in a dimly lit hallway, rain dripping from his coat as he raises a knife. His victim is frozen, the fear in her eyes described in excruciating detail.

I read faster, my heart pounding as the scene unfolds with a clarity I can't grasp. These images aren't in my head—I can't see them, not with the darkness of my aphantasia—but the words... they crawl under my skin, burrowing deep. The level of detail feels too sharp, too specific. Like someone had been there. Like someone had seen it happen.

My pulse roars in my ears as my gaze slowly drifts toward the direction of the bedroom, and the snores coming from within.

Why did Stephen have my manuscript?

More importantly, why did he have it a whole two weeks *early*?

My breathing tightens and I start to hyperventilate. I bend over the kitchen counter, trying to hold back the urge to throw up as I process it all.

It sounds so ridiculous that I can't believe the question even pops into my mind, but could Stephen really be my Charles Dickens?

I shake my head, trying to convince myself that it couldn't possibly. This was a mistake. It *had* to be a mistake.

But I find myself trying to recall exactly when it was that we met. And I realize that it was only a few weeks after my first book hit the best seller list.

I think I'm going to throw up.

I stumble toward the trashcan, and throwing open the lid, I vomit. It comes in three waves, fat tears leaking down from the corner of my eyes. I fall to my knees and start shaking, digging my fingers into my scalp. Then I push myself to my feet and clean my mouth and face.

I don't care that it's the middle of the night, or that Stephen will probably be furious at being woken up. I need answers.

I grab the manuscript and march toward the bedroom, slamming the door open. He jolts awake, looking up at me with bleary, confused eyes.

"What... Luna? What's wrong?"

"What's this?" I demand, holding the envelope up like it's a weapon.

Stephen squints at it, still half-asleep. "Huh?"

"This," I repeat, my voice sharper. "The envelope. Why do you have it?"

"That's what you woke me up for? Really?"

"I'm serious!" I snap. In a slow, sharp voice, I ask, "Where did you get it?"

He shakes his head, rubbing a hand over his face. "You're unbelievable, Luna. Who cares where I got the envelope from? Honestly, you need to get some sleep. You've been staying—"

"Stephen!"

He shuts up, realizing that this wasn't like the other arguments we had. This was important to me. *Very* important.

He lets out a long sigh. "That?" He gestures to the envelope. "It came earlier today and I grabbed it for you."

"It's not supposed to come today," I say. "It's never come this early before. Ever."

"Maybe they're early this time. I don't know, Luna. I didn't exactly ask the mailman for a detailed explanation of why he was delivering a package, now did I?"

My jaw tightens. "You didn't think it was strange? You didn't wonder why it was here now?"

"Luna, it's late," he groans. "It's just a package. Come to bed."

I pause. "You don't know what's inside?"

"Why would I? It's for *you*. I don't open your stuff, you know that."

"You *really* don't know what it is?"

He slowly draws a deep breath, then just as slowly, releases it. "It's heavy, so I don't know. Another one of your edited manuscripts from the editor? What's her name? Janine?"

"Janice."

"Right. Her."

Could he be telling the truth? Maybe. He could be lying too, but I wasn't sure. Stephen had never come across to me like he could be any good at lying.

"Are you going to come to bed now?"

I bite my lip.

"Please?"

"Alright, alright. Let me put this away, then I'm coming."

He breathes a sigh of relief and turns back over into his pillow.

I clutch the envelope to my chest as I step back into the hall, my fingers trembling against the crisp edges. Stephen's snores resume almost immediately, soft and unbothered.

Could it really be nothing? Just an early delivery, a harmless mistake?

I want to believe him. I need to believe him. But the timing gnaws at me, carving a pit in my stomach. And there was the fact that he'd been missing from the house earlier. Where had he gone? It wasn't like Stephen had a ton of friends he'd go regularly meet, nor was he the type to just go off and run errands. He'd always announce to me something like, "Hey, Luna, I'm going shopping. You need anything?"

He was attentive like that. Kind, loving, *thoughtful*.

When I drop the manuscript off onto my desk, my hands linger on the brown envelope, and look back in the direction of the snores. Stephen couldn't be Charles Dickens. He couldn't. It's absurd.

But then again, isn't that how these stories always go?

The helper. The partner. The one you trust the most. The one hiding right under your nose.

I make my way back to the bedroom. Stephen is still, his form a shadow in the muted light of the hallway. For the first time, I don't feel the warmth of familiarity. Instead, he feels like a stranger.

Despite that, I crawl into bed, letting his drifting hands rest on waist. I do my best to sleep. But all I can think about is the nagging feeling that the manuscript sitting on my desk is something much darker than fiction.

ELEVEN

I'd be lying if I said I didn't turn into a paranoid stalker. Every move Stephen made, I watched. How he ate, how he walked, how he scrolled through his phone. When he took calls and stepped into another room, I followed quietly, pressing my ear against the door like some amateur detective in a paperback novel. But every time, I found nothing—nothing suspicious, nothing out of place. Just Stephen being Stephen.

Simple. Loving. Predictable Stephen.

And yet, when he finally cleared my suspicions about the package—explaining, rather plainly, that he'd grabbed it from the mailman on my behalf—I felt something I wasn't expecting. Disappointment. Not relief. Disappointment. The realization hit me like a dull ache in the chest, though I couldn't quite pin down why. Maybe it was the thrill of finally knowing who my Charles Dickens was. Who knows. Whatever the feeling was, it fizzled away into the air.

As for the manuscript, it remained exactly where I

had left it, sitting untouched and unread on my desk. Normally, I would have devoured it by now. The sooner I read through a manuscript, the sooner I could pass it off as my own, slap a polished marketing campaign on it, and watch the royalties pour in. But with this one... I couldn't bring myself to open it. Couldn't face whatever twisted world lay within its pages.

I didn't know why. Then again, I didn't seem to know a whole lot of things these days.

The growing storm online didn't help. Every corner of the internet seemed to buzz with the controversy surrounding Miss Murder. The backlash was a double-edged sword. On the one hand, it was hurting my reputation—authors were pulling away, distancing themselves, refusing to be seen anywhere near my name. I'd been blocked from the online writing groups where I'd once been a star contributor. It was almost funny—half of them owed their success to the marketing tips I'd shared over the years. But loyalty only goes so far when you're accused of profiting off tragedy.

On the other hand, to my surprise, the backlash was fueling sales. People who had never heard of me before were now buying my books in droves, driven by the same morbid curiosity that makes true-crime documentaries trend on Netflix.

Was this author really writing from the killer's perspective? Were these stories based on real crimes?

It didn't matter how loudly people protested or how many hashtags were flung my way—everyone wanted to know. And they were buying my books to find out.

But it wasn't the kind of success I wanted. It wasn't

the kind of success anyone with an ounce of foresight would want. This was fleeting. Toxic. The kind of success that always implodes, leaving nothing behind but ashes and regrets.

At least, I think it is. I'm not sure of anything anymore.

The isolation of it all was starting to get to me. It's one thing to be disliked; it's another to be actively shunned. No one wanted to hear my side of the story, not even the people I thought were my friends. So I did what anyone would do when their world is crumbling—I gave up and sank into the couch, surrounded by an assortment of fatty snacks and a dull lineup of housewives on TV screaming at each other.

The bag of chips crinkles in my lap as I reach for another handful, my eyes glued to the screen. A housewife throws a wine glass, the red liquid spraying in slow-motion across stark white walls. It's ridiculous. I almost laugh at the absurdity of it all. Almost.

But then, a notification dings on my phone, slicing through the haze of my thoughts. My heart stutters, the familiar edge of panic flaring to life. I grab the phone with shaky hands and glance at the screen.

Reminder: Momnt Live in 10 Minutes.

"Shit," I hiss, shoving the chips aside. They tumble to the floor, forgotten, as I scramble off the couch. My foot catches the edge of the coffee table, nearly sending me sprawling, but I don't stop. I sprint to the bathroom, flicking on the light and freezing when I catch sight of myself in the mirror.

Disheveled hair. Smudged mascara. Crumbs dotting my oversized shirt like some humiliating badge of shame.

Miss Murder, the queen of murder thrillers? Hardly.

I yank a hairbrush through the tangles and splashing water on my face. A quick swipe of concealer, a dab of blush, and a touch of my signature red lipstick. My hands shake as I line my eyes, knowing full well it's an uphill battle to make myself look polished in time. But when I stare in the mirror, a passable version of Miss Murder stares back. Not flawless, but polished enough.

I change into something sleek and black—a safe choice for Miss Murder—and hustle to my desk. By the time I sit down and adjust the camera angle, my hands are trembling. The livestream countdown ticks down from ten seconds, and I force a smile as the screen lights up.

"Hello to all of my wonderful fans!" I say, a little breathless. "It's so great to see you all here."

My eyes flick down to the bottom of the screen, where I see a viewer count. It's in the tens of thousands. My mouth suddenly feels quite dry.

But the chat explodes with greetings, a mix of loyal fans and curious newcomers flooding the stream. My practiced smile doesn't falter as I dive into the usual spiel, thanking everyone for their support and hyping up the latest release of *The Broken Boy*. For a brief, shining moment, it feels like old times. Normal.

I absolutely LOVE your books, Luna!

I can't stop reading. How do you do this?!

Going through your backlist, and they're amazing. Just wow.

One by one, the positivity builds. And seeing the comments come in like that, I'm suddenly filled with hope that I can rebuild my brand and that things will be okay.

But then, another comment appears.

What do you have to say about the Val Felder?

The words hit like a punch to the gut, but I keep my smile plastered on. "Great question!" I say, deflecting smoothly. "Let's focus on the new book today. I'm really excited for you all to read it."

Another comment pops up. *Is it true your books are based on real murders?*

Then another. *Why haven't you addressed the claims? Guilty much?*

The floodgates open. My heart pounds as the chat fills with accusations, hashtags, and demands for answers. My usual supporters are drowned out by trolls and skeptics, their voices a rising tide of judgment.

Luna, did you use real murder details in Don't Breathe Twice?

Did you steal a grieving mother's tragedy to sell books?

How do you sleep at night?

My throat tightens, and my carefully constructed mask begins to crack. "I—I really appreciate your questions," I stammer, my voice faltering. "But I can't comment on every rumor out there."

The trolls are relentless.

You're profiting off death.

Disgusting.

Explain the murder details from the alleyway!

Here's a thought. What if she was the one who murdered Cody Felder?

Ice grips my heart. I try to picture the scene they're talking about so that I can answer and give some sort of explanation around the specifics of it. But my aphantasia leaves me blank, there to paralyze me and remind me that *no*, everything is *not* alright.

Tears prick at the corners of my eyes, but I fight to hold them back. This was a mistake. A huge mistake. "I think that's all the time we have for today," I say, my voice barely steady. "Thank you so much for joining—"

The screen freezes for a second as I hit the end button. Then silence.

My reflection stares back at me from the blank screen, eyes glassy and red-rimmed. I slump back in my chair, the weight of the backlash pressing down on me like an iron hand.

Then a notification appears on my screen.

Watch @ValFelder on Momnt

I reach forward, tap the notification, and Val appears on the screen. Heavy tears streak her cheeks, and her chin trembles.

"When I first started down this path, trying to get justice for my son, I knew that there was one certain truth I might have to face."

She pauses.

"I thought... nobody will care. We see that all the time, with all the tragedies happening around the world. We see it because the truth is that nobody *does* care until it happens to them."

For a fleeting moment, I feel the weight of my own

complicity, a pang of guilt that mirrors the mother's grief. Val wasn't wrong. That was how the internet worked. Until now.

"But for some reason, you, the book community, have decided that you cared about *me*, about my son, Cody Felder." Another tear rolls down her cheek, and she shakes her head. "I cannot tell you what that means to me. To know that you share the same feelings that I have. My son does not deserve to have his death written about in some horrible murder thriller. His death should be respected. Not mocked, for the sheer purpose of advancing Luna Harrow's career and the weight of her wallet."

She pauses again, letting the weight of that statement settle in as she stares into the camera. Her stare lingers long enough for chills to travel down my neck and the hairs along my arm to rise.

Her voice changes, dipping lower as she narrows her gaze. "I see you. I know you're watching this. I told you that the whole world will know what you've done. And now they do, Miss Murder."

She leans forward, lips twisting into an ugly snarl.

"Now they do, Luna Harrow." The words are slower, more deliberate. Her lips draw back, revealing her bared teeth. "You *fraud*."

She cuts the livestream, and silence swarms around me. I can't tear my eyes away from the screen. Then something appears at the top, suggested within the search bar.

#LunaHarrowExposed has hit number one for trending topics.

TWELVE

The garden is overgrown, weeds twisting their way through what was once a neat border of lavender and wildflowers. My knees sink into the damp earth as I tug at the tangled mess, each pull sending a jolt through my arms.

The gardener was due to show up this week, but in the aftermath of the Miss Murder controversy, he seems to be missing.

I don't mind, though. The work is mindless, repetitive, exactly what I need right now. Anything to keep my hands busy, to stop my thoughts from circling back to Val Felder and the unread manuscript still sitting on my desk.

As I work, I'm reminded of before the machines, when there were no soft beeps or drones of equipment to mar the silence. When I was a child, sometimes my mother would take me out into the garden. Of course, the garden was significantly smaller than the one I have now.

We'd spend hours out there, and I'd watch my mother with her hands deep in the soil, coaxing life out of the soil with a patience I never understood. She tried to convince me to help her, but I hated it back then—hated the dirt under my nails, the sweat dripping down my back. But now? I dig eagerly into the dirt, doing anything I can to pull life from it.

I'm learning that sometimes, the way to do just that is to get rid of the bad bits. I rip another weed from the ground, before shaking loose the dirt and tossing it into the pile beside me. It's a rhythmic motion that dulls the edges of my thoughts, but not enough. Val's voice still echoes in my head.

You fraud.

One of the weeds in front of me is stubborn, clutching to the earth with its long roots. I dig harder, my gloves caked with soil as I claw at them. The sun is hidden behind the thick clouds, leaving the air cool and damp. It's miserable weather, but my mother would have looked at this weather and with a wide smile, would have said it's the perfect weather for planting. That's the difference between my mother and I. She always found joy in these moments, in the small victories of pruning and planting, watching the garden grow.

I wonder if she'd feel the same if she could see me now, kneeling in the dirt like a desperate child, trying to chase some semblance of control over her life.

The stubborn weed finally gives way under my grip, and I sit back on my heels, breathing heavily. My gaze drifts to the small patch of flowers I managed to save— pale, wilted things clinging to life in the shadow of the overgrowth. The sight makes my chest ache. I don't know why I'm even bothering. It's not like anyone else will see this place. Not like anyone else cares.

I pick up a trowel and start digging into a corner where the soil is compacted, the metal scraping against tiny rocks. My hands are sore, my knees damp and aching, but I don't stop. Not yet. If I stop, the silence will creep back in, and with it, everything I've been trying to ignore.

The notifications. The hashtags. The endless stream of accusations flooding Momnt and every other platform I've ever used. My name is everywhere, tied to tragedy, to greed, to something monstrous. I thought I could outrun it, but the world has a way of catching up.

I wonder if my mother ever felt like this. Probably not. She always seemed so sure of herself, so unshakable. Or maybe she was just better at hiding it.

The trowel slips from my hand, landing in the dirt with a dull thud. I sit back, wiping my forehead with the back of my glove and staring at the mess I've made. The weeds are gone, but the patch looks raw, exposed, like the soil is mourning its loss.

It's strange, how you can pour yourself into something and still feel empty afterward.

I lean forward, my elbows resting on my knees, and let out a long breath. The lake ripples nearby, the wind picking up just enough to send a chill down my spine. Somewhere in the distance, a bird calls out, its cry sharp and lonely. I close my eyes, trying to hold onto the sound, to let it fill the space where everything else feels hollow.

But no matter how hard I try, Val's voice slips

through the cracks, dragging me back to the chaos I'm trying so hard to forget.

I suppose it's time for me to go inside now. There are only so many hours you can spend hiding from everything. Only so many weeds to pluck and pull. I pick myself up and go back into the house without putting away the gardening tools. That could be the gardener's job, now that I've done his for him. That was, if he ever decided to show up again.

When I enter the house and strip off my boots and jacket, I realize that the warmth I expected to feel isn't so warm at all. In fact, it's rather cold.

With a deep frown, I make my way through the house and realize that the front door is slightly open.

Did I leave it open by accident? Or Stephen?

"Stephen?" I call out.

There's no answer. But when I stick my head out the door, I see that his car isn't in the driveway. He probably forgot his wallet inside and didn't shut the door properly the second time. It's happened before. I push on the door, frowning as the door clicks shut. The sound's echoed through the house in an eerie sort of way.

I can't explain it, but my instincts tell me something's wrong. I go into the kitchen and scan the counters, the table, the sink—looking for something, anything, out of place. But everything is just as I left it. The mug from this morning still sits in the sink, a faint coffee ring around the base. The fruit bowl remains untouched, the bananas starting to spot. It all looks normal. But it doesn't feel normal.

"Vincent?" I call out, my voice hesitant this time.

The house remains quiet, except for the faint hum of the refrigerator and the distant sound of my mother's equipment. My chest tightens as I glance toward the hallway leading to my mother's room.

I walk down the hall, each step slower than the last. The door to my mother's room is slightly ajar, and I push it open with trembling fingers. The soft beep of her machines greets me, steady and rhythmic, and to my deep relief, there's not a thing that looks out of place.

My mother's awake, her eyes open and locked onto the ceiling, her hands remaining at her side just as they always do. All the books on the shelves are still perfectly lined. I place a hand over my chest to still my racing heart, and—

What's that?

There's a plain white envelope sitting at the foot of my mother's bed. At first glance, it's so ordinary that it might as well be invisible if you weren't looking for it. But I see it.

I lift it and am surprised to find that it feels almost empty. Holding up to the light, though, I see the truth. There's something inside.

But of course there is. It's an *envelope*, and a perfectly normal looking envelope at that. Except I can't explain it. The feeling that grips me leaves me feeling uneasy.

"Vincent?" I call out again, hoping that he might finally answer and let me know he accidentally left it behind.

There's no answer.

I bite my lip. If it *does* belong to him, then it'd be in

poor taste to open it. Except for the fact that it was left here, on my mother's bed.

Making a decision that opening it was not really that serious, I run my finger under the sealed flap. A small piece of paper slides out and flutters to the ground, landing at my feet.

A single phrase written in bold, slanted letters stares up at me.

RETIRE OR ELSE.

The words blur as my vision tunnels, my pulse roaring in my ears. I snatch the note up, flipping it over to the other side to see if there's been anything else written, but it's just that. I check inside the envelope, almost expecting something worse to fall out—a photo, maybe, or something grotesque. But there's nothing else. Just those three words: retire or else.

Another thought pops into my mind.

Someone was in my house.

I race to the kitchen and pull the biggest knife I can from the drawer, my heart pounding against my ribcage. With the note in one hand and my weapon in the other, I check the rest of the house.

I had thought things couldn't get any worse. But I was so, *so* wrong. I search every corner, every closet, behind every nook and cranny until I'm absolutely sure it's just my mother and me here.

We're safe.

Except that's a lie. The privacy of my home had been shattered by a stranger. There was no feeling safe here anymore. Closing my eyes, fighting the urge to cry, I wish that I could just sell this place and move on with my life.

But there's too much to lose. I couldn't let whoever this was intimidate me.

I wipe my eyes dry and return to my mother. It didn't take two guesses to know what they meant by 'or else'. The threat had been left at my mother's feet for a reason.

I force a smile so she doesn't worry. "Hey mom, are you okay?"

She doesn't answer. That's no surprise. With a jolt, I realize that she probably heard the intruder come in. She might even have seen their face.

"Don't suppose you can tell me who left this letter here for us?" I laugh. The hysteria might be starting to get to me. The note crinkles in my hand as I fold it, slipping it into my pocket. My throat tightens as I sit next to her, stressfully running my hand through my long hair.

I can't tell if I'm shivering because of the cold or because of the way my mind is spiraling. One of the comments from that disastrous livestream pops into my head.

What if she was the one who murdered Cody Felder?

Was it possible that Val had seen that comment and begun to wonder? Could *she* have been the one to break into my home and leave the threat?

No, that didn't feel like her. While I'd felt her anger that night she knocked on my door, even thought she might want to hurt me, I'd never felt in danger of losing my life. Or my mother's, for that matter.

But I'd be foolish to think that it couldn't have been one of her supporters; a fan of mine who probably saw the injustice and thought they should do something about it. Vigilantes were everywhere these days.

Retire.

What does that even mean? Quit writing? Quit breathing?

A bitter laugh escapes my lips before I can stop it. Whoever wrote this doesn't know me. They don't know that fear isn't enough to make me quit. If anything, it makes me dig my heels in deeper. But the laugh dies quickly, replaced by the weight of unease curling in my stomach.

I glance toward the door again, some sixth sense of mine whispering that someone's been watching me. A shadow moves beyond the door, and I jump to my feet with a wild scream, brandishing the knife back and forth.

The door swings open, light spilling through the opening to reveal...

Vincent.

He keeps his hands to the side, so I can clearly see he's not holding a weapon, and his eyes are filled with concern.

"Ms. Harrow?"

I lower the knife and slap a hand over my mouth. "Vincent! I'm so sorry!"

His eyes flick from me to the knife, then to my mother. "Maybe we should talk before you do anything... rash."

For a second, I'm confused as to what he's talking about. But as my eyes lower to the knife and to my mother, I suddenly realize what this looks like.

I can't help it—I start cackling. I'm *definitely* losing it.

"I'm not going to kill my mom, Vincent. I just thought there was someone in the house."

He breathes a sigh of relief and gives me a smile. "Well, it's just me."

"You haven't seen anybody else?" I ask.

"No, but I suppose I just came in. Wasn't Stephen here?"

"Was he?"

"I thought so."

"Oh. Well, he's gone now. I'm not sure where."

A long, piercing beep cuts through the room.

THIRTEEN

"Vincent?" I gasp. "What's happening?"

He doesn't answer right away. Calmly, he strides toward the machine.

I grip the edge of the bed, watching as he leans over the sleek monitor, his fingers flying over the controls with practiced ease. The beep continues, drilling into my skull.

"Is she okay?" I manage, my breath coming in quick, shallow bursts. "Vincent, *is she okay?*"

"It's nothing to worry about," he says smoothly, his tone even. He doesn't look back at me, his focus entirely on the machine. "Just a minor adjustment. These systems are precise—they pick up on even the smallest fluctuations."

His explanation doesn't do much to ease the knot tightening in my chest. My mother's face is as serene as ever, her breathing steady, but my gaze keeps flicking to the machine, as if expecting it to flash some kind of warning in bright red letters.

The beep suddenly stops, and Vincent straightens, glancing over his shoulder at me.

"All sorted," he says. "It was a calibration issue. Happens occasionally. Doesn't it, Madeline?"

My grip on the bed loosens, but the tension lingers. His explanation makes sense—I know these machines are cutting-edge, that every detail of my mother's care is top of the line—but it doesn't stop the sinking feeling in my stomach.

Vincent's eyes flick to me, taking in the way I'm still gripping the bed frame.

"Let's get you a glass of water," he says, already moving toward the door.

I brush my hand over my mother's before following him out of the room. We reach the kitchen and he trades me a glass of water for the knife. He puts it back where it belongs, leans back against the counter, and folds his arms over his chest.

"I know it's not really my place, Ms. Harrow, but something seems wrong."

A huff of air escapes through my lips. Such a light way to put it. How about *everything's* wrong?

I take a drink. Then I ask, "Be honest. Have you heard about the controversy?"

He nods.

"And?"

"People seem to be making trouble out of nothing."

"There's a police report that matches the details in my book, Vincent. That's not exactly nothing. Anyway, I don't have the headspace to talk about all that. That's a whole other issue in itself." I pull the threatening note from my pocket. "I found this at the foot of my mother's bed."

He takes it and unfolds it, his eyes scanning the words.

"Retire or else," he reads aloud. "Odd. Did you see who left it here?"

"No. I thought they might be in the house still, but..."

"That's why you had the knife. And why you were so scared when you saw me."

I nod.

"I see. Is there any chance this could be from Stephen? I know..." he stops speaking, suddenly aware of what he's saying.

"You know what?"

He grimaces and passes me the note. "He's talked about wanting to spend more time with you. How it would be nice if you retired and focused on a life with him."

I gape at him. "Stephen? *He* told you that?"

"You were working late. He was a little drunk. I'm sorry. I was checking on your mother and—"

"It's fine," I cut him short. "I'm just... surprised, is all. Can't believe Stephen would share that with you."

He chuckles, "You mean you can't believe he would talk to me."

I stammer, but he raises a hand.

"I know he is not a big fan of me."

I hesitate, trying to find a different spin on it. In the end, I can't. "I'm sorry."

"Don't be. It's okay. I'm here for different reasons, aren't I?"

"That's true," I answer. I was paying him a significant sum of money to be a full-time carer for my mother. "I suppose it could've been Stephen."

"But?"

"What if it's that grieving mother, Val? Or someone online who decided to take justice into their own hands?" I pose, my voice wavering slightly. I take a long sip of water to steady myself.

Vincent tilts his head slightly as he considers my words. "It's possible," he says after a pause. "But it could also mean nothing. People send threats all the time without any real intention behind them."

"Vincent. It was on my mother's *bed*, with her *in* it."

He doesn't respond right away, and for a moment, I wonder if he's dismissing me. But then he says, "I could take one of the spare bedrooms inside the house, if you like. Near your mother's room, where I can continue to make sure everything stays safe?"

I hesitate, surprised he'd make the offer. It would solve at least this one thing, having another person I trusted inside the house. "You'd do that?"

He shrugs, "Until whatever this is blows over, absolutely."

I throw my arms around him, so beyond grateful that some of the weight is off my shoulders. It was one thing trying to navigate this mess between me, Val, and all of my readers. It was another trying to make sure my own home was safe.

I'd need to have a conversation with Stephen. I know he wouldn't love the idea of another man living under my own roof, but he would understand once I told him about the note. He was thoughtful like that.

"Thank you," I whisper.

His arms tighten slightly around me, and for a moment, I allow myself to lean into him. He smells good—clean, with a soft touch of amber and oud—and I realize just how tense I've been, how much I needed this small, fleeting comfort. There's a strength to him, lean but solid, the kind of strength that makes you feel safe even when everything's coming down around you.

Something warm bubbles up inside me, spreading through my chest, chasing away the chill that's been clinging to me ever since that horrible woman knocked on the door. It feels good. Too good. My breathing slows, matching the rhythm of his, and I can feel his heartbeat faintly against my temple.

The hug lingers a moment too long, and the air shifts between us. Tighter. Heavier. My hands curl slightly against his back, and I feel him exhale, his breath warm against my hair.

Then, as if on cue, we step away at the same time.

Vincent gives me a calm smile, so easy, so natural, like nothing happened. Like I wasn't just pressed against him, noticing the way his body felt, how solid and reassuring he was.

He nods toward the hallway. "I'll grab my things from the guesthouse. You should get cleaned up and go out for a bit. Get some fresh air. Maybe you'll get some ideas about all the controversy? I'll stay here and keep an eye on Madeline."

I blink at him. "You... you don't mind?"

"Of course not. Go clear your head. You've got a lot going on." His voice is steady, kind, but professional. Detached, almost.

"Right," I say, nodding slowly. "That's... that's probably a good idea."

He's already moving toward the door, his steps measured and slow. "Take your time," he calls over his shoulder. "I'll be here."

The door clicks shut behind him, and I'm left standing in the kitchen, trying to make sense of what just happened. It was just a hug. Just a moment of gratitude. Nothing more.

Nothing more.

And yet, I can still feel the press of his arms, the warmth of his body, the way his heart thudded against his chest, against *me*. I shake my head, trying to dismiss the thought. No, that couldn't be, because nothing happened.

I glance toward the door, conscious of how Stephen's car wasn't in the driveway. A part of me feels relief that he wasn't here to see this, to misinterpret what was just a fleeting, innocent gesture.

Still, I can't help but feel... confused. About what? I don't even know. When I head to the bathroom and get into the shower, I choose to let the cold water run over me, washing the sweat and mud away, hoping that it'd be enough to cool the heat coursing through me. But when I step out and wrap a towel around myself, I can still smell him, even still feel the touch of his fingers on me.

My phone sits on the bathroom counter, its screen

dark and free of the notifications that had haunted me as of late. I'd muted them for today in an attempt to free up space in my mind. Couldn't exactly breathe with the accusatory comments, posts, videos, and livestreams all tagging me, each clamoring for attention to say, *I was on Val's side.*

I reach for my phone, wondering where Stephen was. It'd be great to ask him and see if he really was the one who left the note behind on my mother's bed. If so, then we had things to talk about. I wasn't mad, really. I could understand how difficult things must be for him. But still, he had to know that he *could* speak to me, without resorting to ridiculous letters that did nothing but heighten my fears.

I bite my lips, feeling guilty for more reasons than one. I'd let this controversy isolate me from him, and I didn't want to lose him. Maybe he was right. I hadn't opened up enough to him.

I send him a text.

Hey, want to get a bite to eat?

Waiting for him to respond, I blow-dry my hair and dry myself off, getting changed into a comfortable pair of clothes that I could go out in. I have no doubt that #LunaHarrowExposed is trending as hot as ever, but I'm beginning to realize that sitting around, letting myself get caught up in it all won't give me room enough to breathe and think of a solution that might finally put it all to bed without *completely* ruining Miss Murder.

I check my phone. Still unread.

I scoff, rolling my eyes, but guilt presses against my chest. Was I being unfair? Probably. I should message him back, apologize for how distant I've been, and for accusing him so late at night about the manuscript. But the thought of starting that conversation feels exhausting, and to be honest, I'm not sure I'm up for it now. I'm not sure I'm up for anything, besides the warmth of a cappuccino between my hands.

Slipping my phone into my pocket, I leave the house and get into my Range Rover. Ten minutes later, I pull into a spot and notice a familiar vehicle up ahead.

I squint to get a better look at the license plate. It's Stephen's. Why is Stephen here? I have never seen him drink a coffee, let alone visit a café by himself.

My mouth dips into a frown. My heels click against the pavement as I walk toward the café, hating the prickle at the back of my neck.

This is *Stephen*. Maybe he was grabbing me a coffee as a surprise. I mean, I'm sure I must have mentioned how much I loved this place to him before. Or maybe he'd seen a receipt of mine floating around somewhere. There were plenty of explanations, reasons for why he would be here, getting—

Janice.

Seeing her through the café window twists my stomach. She's sitting at *our* table. And sitting across from her, his head tilted toward hers, is Stephen.

They're leaning in close, their foreheads almost touching as they speak. I can't see their faces from where I'm standing, but there's no mistaking it. This is *not* the first time they've met. They seem far too familiar with one another for this to be just a casual encounter. No, this is something else.

A dozen thoughts flash through my mind, each one worse than the last. Why are they here together? Why didn't Janice tell me she was meeting him? And why, why does this feel so... intimate?

An affair.

The word slams into me, unbidden and unwelcome. My chest tightens as I watch, trying to reconcile what I'm seeing with what I know—or thought I knew—about Stephen and Janice. He's never mentioned her. She's never mentioned him. None of this makes sense. Stephen doesn't even really know her name. And yet, here they are, sitting together at my table.

I can't move. My feet feel glued to the pavement as my mind races, trying to wrap my head around it. Stephen doesn't even drink coffee. And Janice—she's professional to a fault. This is breaking *routine*.

Unless it isn't.

I feel the first prick of tears in my eyes and blink them back furiously. A sharp breeze cuts through the air, sending a shiver down my spine. I step back, then again, my heels clicking against the pavement. They still don't notice me, too caught up in their little bubble. I turn quickly, heading back to my car, my breath coming fast and shallow.

My thoughts spiral as I fumble with my keys, climbing into the driver's seat and slamming the door behind me. My hands grip the steering wheel so tightly my knuckles ache.

It feels like my whole life is breaking into a million puzzle pieces, none willing to fit back together, each jagged and sharp enough to make me bleed.

I throw the car into reverse and peel out, tires screeching. I don't know where I'm going, only that I can't stay here. Not with the creeping, suffocating suspicion that I'm losing control of everything—including the people I thought I could trust most.

FOURTEEN

I don't go straight home. I drive, and drive, and drive, hoping that the thought would somehow scrape itself from my mind. But instead, when I pull up into my driveway and my tires crunch against the gravel, that same thought is branded into my mind.

My Stephen—my kind, thoughtful, *loving* Stephen—was having an affair with my editor.

I sit in the car for a long while, the leather of the steering wheel smooth beneath my hands. I stare at the house, not wanting to go inside, and it has nothing to do with the insidious manuscript sitting unread on my desk. Instead, it has everything to do with him. I just know that when I go inside, I'll smell him. I'll see him and all of his things everywhere I look.

It's tempting, the feeling to just throw the car into reverse, back out of the driveway, and just leave all of this behind. After all, I had enough money in my account to start over somewhere. *Anywhere*, really. There were plenty of places full of people who didn't know that Miss

Murder or Luna Harrow even existed, and better yet, they were full of people who *weren't* Stephen.

Truthfully, I would have done it if it weren't for my mother. As awful as my problems were, she still needed me. I couldn't just leave.

A deep sigh escapes me as I climb out of the car and slam the door shut, the sound echoing through the quiet.

The front door creaks open, and Vincent appears, frowning as he looks at me. "Ms. Harrow? You're back already? I thought you were—

"I don't want to talk about it," I say, brushing past him.

His expression shifts, surprise flickering across his face. "Did something happen?"

I don't answer. My eyes land on Stephen's things. The jacket draped over the back of the chair, the bag he never bothers to put away. How could I have ever felt guilty for not giving him the attention he deserved, when he was cheating on me behind my back?

The thought leaves a sour taste in my mouth, and before I know it, I'm reaching for his things. I grab them all in one swift motion, my grief shifting into rage.

"Ms. Harrow—" Vincent starts, stepping forward, but I'm already moving toward the door.

"These don't belong here anymore," I say, my voice sharp and trembling. I throw the door open and toss the items onto the front lawn, the jacket landing in a heap on the grass, the bag's contents spilling out onto the gravel.

Vincent hesitates, his eyes narrowing slightly as he watches me. "Do you want to talk about—"

"No," I cut him off. "I don't."

I turn back into the house. My gaze lands on more of Stephen's things—a pair of shoes by the door, his mug on the counter, the book he's been reading on the coffee table. I grab them all, and throw them out. I'm breathless as I yank his clothing from the hangers and pull his pillow from the bed. I throw them out too, forming a pile of a cheater's belongings on the driveway.

"Ms. Harrow, maybe you should take a moment to—"

"I don't need a moment!" I shout, my voice breaking. "I need all of this gone. I need *him* gone."

The words echo in the silence, and for a moment, neither of us moves. My hands are shaking. The rage and hurt are twisting together into something I can't control.

And then the sound of tires crunching against the gravel reaches my ears. I whip around, my breath catching as Stephen's car pulls into the driveway. He steps out, his face a mix of confusion as he looks at the mess on the lawn, then at me.

"Luna, what's going on?" he asks, his eyes filled with genuine concern.

Even now as I stare at him, I struggle to reconcile with the fact that this man was a fox, a cheat, a two-faced snake who'd sought his own pleasure instead of caring about *me*.

"What's going on?" I repeat, my voice trembling with anger. "I saw you!"

"You saw me? What's that supposed to mean?"

"Don't play games with me, Stephen. I saw you with Janice, at the café."

His eyes drift toward the things on the ground, then

back to me. Something clicks in his eyes, and I see the moment that he realizes that I know.

His eyes widen, his hand instinctively going up as if to defend himself. "Luna, I—"

"Save it," I snap, my chest heaving. "I don't want to hear your excuses. I don't want to hear *anything* from you, Stephen. We're done."

"Wait—" he starts, stepping closer, but I hold up a hand, stopping him in his tracks.

"I said we're done," I say. The tears are threatening to spill, but I refuse to let them. Not here. Not now, while he still stands in front of me. "Take your stuff and go."

He stares at me, his mouth opening as if to say something, but he doesn't. Instead, he turns and heads back to his car, leaving his things behind.

"Wait," I say.

He pauses, glances back at me with hope in his eyes.

I withdraw the folded note from my pocket.

Retire or else.

I don't think so, Stephen.

"I'm not retiring. Miss Murder's got a whole lot more books on the way."

I toss the threat into the air. The note flutters in the breeze, twisting and spinning before landing near Stephen's feet. He stares at it, his eyes narrowing as the written words sink in. The tension in his jaw tightens, and for a moment, I think he's going to say something, to deny everything, to defend himself.

But he doesn't.

His eyes crinkle slightly at the corners, not with guilt, not with sorrow, but something unreadable, something that makes the back of my neck prickle. Slowly, he bends down and picks up the note. He doesn't look at me, doesn't ask questions, doesn't explain.

Instead, he folds the note neatly, his fingers pressing the edges into crisp lines. Then, without a word, he turns, walking back to his car with the same quiet resolve that used to make me think he was steady and dependable. Now it feels like something else entirely—like resignation.

The car door opens and slams shut. The engine roars to life, and he backs out of the driveway, the tires crunching over gravel as he turns onto the street. The red glow of his taillights lingers, burning into my vision until he disappears around the corner.

And just like that, he's gone.

I stand there for a long moment, staring at the empty space where his car was. For the first time in a long time, I suddenly feel like I'm back in control of my life. Energy surges through me, and I know, somehow, that I can handle Val Felder and everyone else.

But first, there's a manuscript waiting on my desk for me.

As I start back toward the house, I look up and realize that Vincent is still standing in the doorway.

"Ms. Harrow," he says quietly. "Are you sure—"

"Yes," I say, cutting him off. "I'm sure."

He nods, his gaze shifting to where Stephen's car once was. "Alright."

I head to my office and the door clicks shut behind me. My leather chair welcomes me, and so does the typewritten manuscript. The first few sentences call out to me.

The night was dark. No moon, no stars, nothing. Maybe they hid, so that they would not have to witness another bloody murder.

I'm sucked into the story, but a feeling lingers in the pit of my stomach. I can't shake the feeling that I've just stepped off a cliff—and there's no telling how far I'll fall.

FIFTEEN

The manuscript doesn't let me go.

Page after page pulls me deeper, its world dark and unrelenting. The words grip me like a vice, refusing to loosen their hold. It's been two days already, and when I glance at the clock, the red numbers flash back at me—1:42 a.m of the next day.

I shake my head in disbelief. I should go to bed, but then I remind myself that there is nobody waiting in it for me. Not anymore. I sigh and return to the book, letting the final chapter suck me in.

My stomach twists as I continue to read, blown away by every turn of the page. It's darker than the others, far darker, but undeniably brilliant. The readers will love it. That is, if I can get them to stop screaming about *Don't Breathe Twice*. I reach the last line of the manuscript, and feel a deep sense of satisfaction.

This will be the book to shut them up.

It has to.

I close the manuscript and set it on the desk, the

leather chair groaning as I lean back. My fingers drum against the armrest as I stare at the neat stack of pages. My readers will devour it. I have no doubt about that.

I pick up my phone and see a countless stream of notifications waiting for me. Tags in videos, comments, and messages all pushing for me to make an official statement; something that explained the ties between the death of Val's son and the details of my book. But as I switch to a financial dashboard that shows my sales over the last week, I see that they're actually higher than ever.

I should feel triumphant. Vindicated. But instead, there's a hollow ache in my chest, because they're not my words. They never have been.

I sigh, rubbing my temples as the thought sinks in. There's no use dwelling on it now. The words come to me, always on time, always for me to publish. That's what matters. That's all that matters.

But not everything is so dependable.

Janice.

In the beginning when I retained her fully for her time, I worried that she might cheat on me with other authors, trying to stack up her client base and income. But I never imagined that she would cheat on me with my *boyfriend*.

My fingernails dig into my palm. They dig so deep that it feels like they're close to drawing blood when I realize that in order to get this newest manuscript out as soon as possible, I would have to work with her. There simply was no time to find and qualify another editor, and given the nature of my situation—the strangely typewritten manuscripts, the quick turnaround times required, the controversy behind Miss Murder—I had a feeling that was impossible to do inside of even two months.

A curse spills out from my mouth as I stand and pace the room. The heat and the anger build up inside me, until I let out a scream and punch the wall.

The anger disappears instantly as I cradle my hand to my chest, biting my lip against the throbbing pain.

Such an *idiot* thing to do.

Nobody would believe that I finished writing whole books as quickly as I did if I had a broken hand. I head straight for the kitchen and get an icepack.

The ice pack presses against my knuckles, the cold numbing the sharp throb of pain. I lean against the counter, a glass of water untouched in front of me. The quiet of the house wraps around me. It's broken only by the soft hum of my mother's machines in the background.

Footsteps echo softly down the hallway, drawing my attention. Vincent appears, his figure illuminated by the hallway light. He stops short when he sees me, his expression unreadable. For a moment, the only sound is the soft crackle of ice shifting in my pack.

Damp dark hair clings to his forehead. He's wearing shorts that stop midway down his thighs, highlighting the strong, lean musculature of his legs, and a ribbed tank top that hugs his shoulders and chest. A light sheen of sweat glistens on his skin, catching the dim light. I blink, my eyes trailing over him in a way I don't mean to.

Vincent notices. He looks down at himself, then back at me, and he chuckles. "Sorry, Ms. Harrow. I'd gone out for a run and forgot my phone in your mother's room. I was just about to shower and get some sleep."

"You're running this late?" The words come out sharper than I mean them to, more to distract myself than anything else.

"Yeah, it's the best time to run."

"But why?"

He shrugs. "I like how dark and quiet it is at night. Means there's nobody around."

I nod, though my thoughts are snagged on the way the shadows dance along the ridges of his arms. Realizing I'm staring, I clear my throat and force a smile. "It's fine. Don't worry. Wear whatever you want. Go naked, for all I care."

The words are out before I can stop them, and the second they leave my mouth, I freeze. A flush creeps up my neck, burning its way to my cheeks as I quickly look away.

Vincent raises an eyebrow, a slow, amused grin spreading across his face. "I'll keep that in mind."

I groan inwardly, shaking my head. "Forget I said that. It's late, I'm tired, and clearly, I'm not thinking straight."

He doesn't push, just gives a quiet laugh and steps toward the door. "Fair enough. I'll head to sleep now, Ms. Harrow. You should get some rest, too."

As he moves past me, I find my voice again. "Vincent," I say, stopping him in his tracks.

He turns, his expression open, his brow raised slightly.

"Stop calling me Ms. Harrow," I say, my voice softer now. "You're living in my house. It's just silly."

For a moment, he doesn't respond, his gaze steady on mine. Then he nods. "Alright, Luna," he says simply, his tone carrying a faint warmth that I don't quite know how to interpret..

I nod back, unsure of what else to say. It's a bit strange hearing my name come from his mouth, after having heard "Ms. Harrow" from him ever since I hired him. That was over two years ago now, just after I bought this house with the money and success of that first book.

He leaves, and a minute or two later, I hear the soft click of his door. I check my hand. It's looking swollen. I sigh, before making my way back to the office.

The manuscript waits for me on my desk, calling to me like it's desperate to be published. Before I can stop myself, I make a decision.

I'll go to Janice's house. I'll hand it to her in person, see if she's got anything to say to my face about Stephen.

The manuscript fits nicely back into the brown envelope it came in, locking away the scent of ink. She had to know that I'd left Stephen now, that I would know about their affair. Would she deny it? Laugh it off? Or would she confess, offer some pitiful, hollow apology that I won't believe?

The thought makes my chest tighten as I set the manuscript aside. I down the rest of my glass in one gulp and go to bed, dreading the long, sleepless night ahead.

I'm sitting outside Janice's house, parked in my Range Rover with the engine idling softly. The brown envelope sits in my lap, my fingers gripping the edges so tightly that the typewritten pages inside must be starting to crease. As much as I want to get out and face her, my body won't cooperate.

She's in there. I know she is. Hiding, probably, behind those pale gray curtains, knowing full well I'd come.

I glance at her house, small but meticulously kept. The shutters are freshly painted white, framing windows that don't let much in. The flowerbeds are neat and symmetrical. If you didn't know what kind of snake lived inside, you'd call it cozy.

Another five minutes crawl by, and I feel the suffocating grip of my own hesitation tightening around my chest.

Just get out, Luna. Just get out and knock.

A car pulls into the neighbor's driveway, breaking the quiet. I glance over to see a woman stepping out, her purse slung over one arm as she pauses to stare at my car. Her gaze is sharp, her brow furrowing as she assesses me. I can practically hear her thoughts. *Who's that? What are they doing here?*

I close my eyes and let out a long, frustrated sigh. The last thing I need right now is for her to call the cops. I know what the headlines would be.

Miss Murder Sitting Outside Stranger's House. Another Murder Thriller on the Way?

The thought almost makes me laugh. Almost. As if I could find inspiration here, in the neatly trimmed lawn of a cheating editor's suburban facade. No, this isn't inspiration. This is confrontation.

I grind my teeth, correcting myself. This isn't confrontation either. This is the simple, professional passing of a manuscript that needs editing. Any punching of any faces would have to happen later, once I've found an editor decent enough to replace her.

I curse. Why did Janice have to be so good at her job?

The neighbor lingers for a moment longer, then heads inside, her front door closing with a sharp click. The street is silent again, except for the faint rumble of my engine and the racing of my thoughts.

Enough. Enough waiting, enough second-guessing, enough letting Janice hold the cards.

I'm Miss Murder. I own the narrative.

I shut off the engine and step out of the car with the manuscript tucked under my arm. The cool morning air nips at my skin as I close the door behind me and start up the driveway.

I'm not sure why, but the house feels different up close. It feels smaller, almost claustrophobic. The paint's a little too clean, and the flowerbeds are a little too perfect.

I push the feeling aside as I reach the door and raise my hand to knock. I hesitate for just a second. What if she's watching me right now, peeking through those curtains, laughing to herself, thinking, *I slept with her boyfriend, and she's still bringing me her manuscript.*

The thought burns. But there's nothing I can do about it.

I knock, my knuckles rapping sharply against the

wood. I can hear the sound echo beyond the door. I straighten myself as I wait, pursing my lips as the seconds slowly pass.

No answer.

I knock again, almost hammering the door with the side of my fist, not caring that the neighbor might hear me.

The seconds drag into minutes, and still, there is nothing. The house is silent.

I step up to the window, trying to peer inside. It's hard to see much. The lights are off. Maybe nobody's home.

But then I catch the flicker of a shadow.

She's avoiding me. She knows I'm here, and she's hiding like a coward. My anger flares hot and fast.

"Open up, Janice!" I shout.

She doesn't. She thinks that she can have an affair with Stephen and that I'll just go away. But I won't. I shove myself against the door and twist the doorknob, like it'll just—

The door swings wide open, and I trip over the doorstep, landing flat on my hands and knees. A hiss escapes my mouth as a fresh wave of pain shoots through my body. I look up and realize that the door had been unlocked. That was a bit strange. What's the point of hiding and pretending you're not home if someone can just open your front door?

I stand, dusting myself off and straightening my clothes, before I retrieve my manuscript. It's still dark inside, shadows hugging every corner of the living room I'm in. Just like the outside of her house, it's meticulously clean and organized. I don't see a single cup or plate left out. Even the TV remote is sitting perfectly next to a Dior magazine on the coffee table. And staring at that magazine, I know it's never been read. Shoot, it's probably never even been opened, judging by how flat the cover rests.

"Janice?" I call out, shutting the door behind me. I flip the switch to the side of the door and start to relax as light floods the room. "You can come out now. I'm not going to kill you."

But I hear nothing. Not a single shift of the floorboards, or the sharp, tight breathing of someone trying to hide, or even the quiet hum of the refrigerator. There's not a single sound that penetrates the silence.

I frown, adjusting the thick envelope under my arm and stepping further into the house.

"Janice?" I call out again, my voice louder this time. It echoes faintly through the house, the sound bouncing off the pristine walls. Still, there's no answer. Just silence. Too much silence.

I shift the envelope under my arm, my footsteps muffled by the plush beige rug beneath me as I move deeper into the living room. The meticulous cleanliness is starting to feel suffocating, like I've stepped into a staged home instead of one that's actually lived in. There's not a speck of dust on the glossy surfaces, not a single smudge on the mirror above the mantle. It's so perfect, it's unnatural.

"Come on, Janice," I mutter under my breath, moving past the couch toward the hallway that stretches into the back of the house. "I know you're here. I'm not here to talk about... Stephen. I just have a manuscript that needs editing."

The air grows cooler the farther I go, each step pulling me deeper into the strange, sterile quiet. The hallway is narrow, the walls lined with framed photos. Perfectly centered, of course. I glance at one as I pass—Janice at some awards event, holding a glass of champagne.

I pass a door that's cracked open, and pause. A faint unease prickles the back of my neck as I smell something... familiar.

Ink.

I gently push on the door and it swings open to reveal steps leading down into darkness. It's a basement. And it looks like the kind of place that someone would take you to harvest your organs. I want to turn away, but the smell of ink is stronger now—so strong that I can't imagine that the smell is just a remnant of the manuscripts I'd shared with her. Taking out my phone, I switch on the light and shine it down the steps. Step by slow, creaking step, I descend.

Truth be told, I'm not sure what I expected. But it wasn't a study. Bookshelves lined the walls, every bookshelf crammed with copies of hardbacks and paperbacks.

I run my fingers along their spines as I walk, reading title after title. There's no pattern to them, no grouping of genre or anything like that. My eyes catch on a book written by Charles Dickens, before passing along to the others. For some vain reason, I search for my own among them. But there are none.

Didn't she have any pride at all that she was the

editor on the most popular books over the last two years? Most of these were by authors that I'd never even heard of. Why exclude my books?

The answer comes to me a moment later. Maybe she felt guilty for sleeping with my boyfriend, and didn't want to see my name every time she stepped down here into her safe space.

I scoff. No, I doubt that. It's more likely that she is jealous and hates me, wanting as little to do with me as possible. I was there to pay her bills and nothing more.

My attention shifts to the desk shoved into the corner at the back of the study. Its surface is empty except for a neat stack of blank papers resting perfectly parallel to the edge.

I frown as I move closer, realizing that the scent is growing stronger. This must be where she edits my books. My fingers brush over the papers, and for a moment, I half-expect to see a manuscript. But they're blank. Just loose sheets of clean, white paper.

Then I see it. The edge of something tucked beneath the desk, just barely visible in the dim light of my phone. My breath catches as I set the brown envelope aside, my fingers reaching down with a hesitant, trembling urgency.

The handle is cold under my touch, and I grunt as I pull the object free, its unexpected weight making me stagger slightly. I set it on the desk with a dull thud, the metallic sheen of its surface catching the light. It looks like a bricfcase, but thicker—bulkier—and there's something staining the edges.

Blood.

The dark, rusty streaks are unmistakable. My

stomach turns, bile rising in my throat as I trace the pattern with my eyes. I swallow hard, my hands shaking as I reach for the twin brass latches. They click open with a sound that echoes through the silence, louder than it should be, like the house itself is holding its breath.

The lid protests with a gentle scrape as I lift it, my phone's beam catching on the contents inside.

A typewriter.

It's black, sleek, its edges worn smooth with use, but polished to a near-perfect shine. The keys gleam, each letter etched with a precision that borders on reverence. A fresh sheet of paper is loaded into the carriage, perfectly aligned, as if someone had left it there, waiting for me.

My fingers hover over the keys, itching to press them, to hear the sharp clack that would fill the room. But I don't. I can't. My attention shifts to the mesh pouch inside the lid, stuffed with crumpled pages and stained clippings that make my blood run cold.

They're crime articles.

The bold headlines scream at me, even as the ink smudges and stains blur the text.

Unsolved Murders Plague Small Town.
Police Seek Leads in Missing Woman's Case.
Family of Disabled Victim Demands Justice.

But it's not just ink. My light reveals dark smears of red on the edges of the clippings. My throat tightens, a shudder running through me I reach for one of the clippings.

The paper crinkles under my touch as I unfold it. My phone's light illuminates a photo of a smiling boy, his face framed by grainy text. The caption below it reads: *Cody Felder, Age 22*.

The breath leaves my lungs in a rush, my hand tightening around the article. Cody Felder. Val Felder's son. My vision blurs as I scan the article.

This wasn't coincidence. This wasn't some clever use of publicly available police reports. The details in *Don't Breathe Twice*—the alley, the timing, the way the boy's body was left—weren't inspired by unsolved murders.

They *were* the murders.

Cold, dark claws grip my heart as my gaze returns to the Charles Dickens book on the shelf. My Charles Dickens, the mysterious ghostwriter who had delivered these twisted stories into my hands and gave me a life I never could've imagined, wasn't some faceless genius typing away in anonymity. It was Janice.

And Janice didn't just write about murders.

She committed them.

I stagger back from the desk. The typewriter sits there, almost like it's smiling at me. Every book I'd ever published, every grisly, horrifying detail that they'd contained, they weren't fiction. They weren't the product of some dark imagination. They were real.

Janice had murdered people. And I—I had published her work, profited from it, built my name and my career on the blood of her victims.

A strangled sound escapes me, half gasp, half sob, as the truth solidifies in my mind. My knees buckle, and I grip the edge of the desk to steady myself, my chest hitching with ragged breaths.

I thought the controversy online was bad already.

What would happen when they began to connect the dots with even more of my books? What would happen when they all collectively realized that these murders had only one thing in common.

Me.

I squeeze my eyes shut, my heart hammering in my chest as I prayed that this was all a nightmare, and that at any moment, I'd wake up. But when I open them again, the scene hasn't changed. It's still there. It's real.

And so are the murders.

The stairs creak behind me.

My heart jumps up into my throat and I spin around, shining the light, nearly pissing myself with fear.

"Janice?"

She doesn't answer, but I know someone's there. When I was outside and looking through the window, I'd seen a shadow. I'm *sure* of it. I move slowly to the stairs, afraid of what I'd see. But when I shine my light up them, I don't see anything. The door is just as I left it.

My light begins to waver as my hands start to shake.

"Janice?" I call out again, my voice cracking with fear. Nobody answers, but I know someone's there. There's no way to explain it, except that I can *feel* their presence.

I realize that I'm still holding the manuscript, the brown envelope crinkled under my grip. It feels absurd, holding onto it now, like it's some kind of shield. But I can't let go. My fingers won't uncurl.

Something groans under pressure again, and my pulse skyrockets, every nerve in my body screaming at me to run. I scramble up the stairs, screaming and howling the whole way, hoping that the loudness of my voice will startle whoever it is just long enough for me to make my escape.

My legs carry me forward, through the living room, past the perfectly arranged coffee table and the untouched Dior magazine, toward the front door.

I twist the knob with trembling hands, throwing the door open and stumbling out onto the porch with panting breaths. The cool morning air hits me like a slap, sharp and biting against my sweat-dampened skin.

That *presence* still feels like it's so close to me, like it's right on my heels. I don't even look back as I race toward my Range Rover and yank the car door open. I slam it shut with enough force that I can feel the glass rattle.

A moment later, the engine roars to life and I don't hesitate.

The tires screech as I back out, gravel spraying like a warning shot. The second I hit the road, I shift into drive, and then I'm gone.

SIXTEEN

It's not until I get home and lock myself in my office that I feel safe again. Or at least, as safe as I can feel, knowing that my editor is a serial killer.

The uneasy feeling of being watched fades slightly, but it doesn't disappear. It clings to me like a shadow, curling around the edges of my thoughts, refusing to let go. Things are worse now. So much worse. Before, with Val Felder on my case, I'd worried about losing my career. My reputation. My readers. But now? Now, I'm working with a killer, and if the world found out, there's no way anyone would believe I had no idea.

I freeze, staring out the window into the dark, empty street. It's quiet outside. My reflection stares back at me, and a thought comes to mind.

If it all came out, they'd stick me in a jail cell.

I don't know how long the sentence would be, but it wouldn't matter. A judge would take one look at the evidence, at the books I've published, at the way each gruesome detail matches the murders, and they'd throw the book at me. Maximum term. A life sentence. Maybe worse.

They'd want to make an example of me.

I press my hand to the glass, the coolness biting into my skin, and try to picture prison bars replacing the window panes. But nothing comes. My aphantasia leaves me with nothing but blackness, the same empty void that's always been there. The one I thought I'd escaped by publishing these stories.

I lean my head against the glass, letting out a heavy sigh. Could it get any worse than that?

My eyes snap open, a chill racing down my spine.

Of course it could.

There's no way Janice would let herself get caught. She's too smart for that, too careful. No, if the world started connecting the dots, she'd need someone to take the fall. And who better than me? The face of Miss Murder. The so-called author profiting off these gruesome crimes.

My stomach twists as the realization settles over me. She'd pin it *all* on me, and the world would want it to be true.

The Life of a Real Serial Killer—Miss Murder.

It's the perfect headline. The kind of story the media would salivate over. True-crime podcasts would dissect every detail, online forums would explode with speculation, and Netflix would have the documentary queued up before the ink on the charges even dried.

I can already hear the narration in my head. *She wasn't just writing about the murders. She was living them.*

The thought makes me groan, the sound escaping before I can stop it. I drop into my chair, pressing my palms to my temples as if I can physically block the thoughts from crawling their way in. But they don't stop. They never stop. Each one is worse than the last, dragging me deeper into the spiraling nightmare I've found myself in.

What's stopping her from going even further?

The question slithers into my mind like a snake, coiling tightly around my chest, squeezing the air from my lungs. What if Janice doesn't just want to frame me? What if she wants to silence me completely?

A shiver shoots through me, sharp and cold, as the thought takes root. She's already proven she's capable of anything. She's already betrayed me once. And now she has every reason to get rid of me—permanently.

She took Stephen from me. That betrayal alone is unforgivable. But now, as I sit here with my hands trembling against the desk, I realize just how much power she holds over me.

And how easily she could take it all away.

The chime of my phone slices through the silence, making me jump. My heart lurches as I grab it, my fingers fumbling over the screen. A new message on Momnt.

From Charles Dickens.

The air feels heavier, like it's pressing down on me. My blood turns cold, my pulse hammering so loudly that it drowns out everything else. My thumb hovers over the notification, hesitation freezing me in place.

Before, I wouldn't have thought twice about opening his messages. Why would I? My Charles Dickens had swooped in and saved me. He'd saved my mother's life, my career, everything.

I grimace as I correct myself. It wasn't *his* charity. It was *her* charity.

The smart thing to do would be to take this phone, take everything I know, and go straight to the police. Get ahead of it all before Val, the fans, or worse, Alyssa Lake, decided to connect the dots themselves.

But I don't do the smart thing.

Instead, my thumb moves on its own, tapping the message. I have to know what she's said. I *have* to.

The words hit me like a punch to the gut:

You shouldn't have gone there.

A chill runs down my spine. Was that a threat? My fingers hover over the keyboard before I force myself to type something, anything, to fill the void in my head.

I was bringing a manuscript, I write back, as if that somehow explains everything. As if that somehow makes this *normal*.

I wait, staring at the screen, willing Janice to respond. To tell me exactly how this is going to play out if I want to stay alive. But there are no dots. No response. Just the crushing silence of being left on read.

I send another message, my fingers trembling as I type.

Tell me I'm crazy. Tell me I'm misinterpreting things, that you didn't commit all those murders.

Three dots appear. I hold my breath, my chest tightening painfully as the seconds crawl by.

I did.

The words slam into me. It's one thing to think it. It's another thing to see her confession typed out so casually.

I'm about to type back when another message comes through.

I murdered them for you.

My stomach flips, a strangled sound escaping me as I bite the back of my fist to keep from screaming. I read it over and over again, hoping it will somehow mean something different the next time. But it doesn't.

Why? I type, my thumbs moving frantically over the screen.

Her response comes quickly, too quickly.

You needed help. You needed stories. I gave them to you.

I'm shaking so badly that it's hard to type.

But I didn't need you to KILL people for me!!! What if people find out?

My message hangs there, sent and waiting, as I chew on my fingernails, my breaths coming in short, shallow bursts. The dots appear again.

I'm so *stupid*. A stupid, desperate fool for accepting the help of a complete stranger from the internet. In what world does any normal person agree to pass over manuscript after manuscript without asking for payment?

Her response is short, like a blade cutting through my thoughts.

They won't.

I shake my head. She doesn't understand how this works. Social media. These people. They can find out anything. They'll dig and dig until they're absolutely sure there are no more skeletons hiding in my closet.

I want to scream, to throw my phone across the room, but my fingers keep moving. Before I can send anything, another message appears.

Stick to our routine. Don't question the process.

The room feels colder as I stare at the screen, my hands trembling, my mind spinning. Stick to the routine? That's what she wants me to do? After everything?

A knock at the door startles me so badly that my phone slips from my hands, the screen cracking as it hits the floor.

"Shit," I hiss, scrambling to pick it up. The fractures spiderweb across the glass, making the messages barely legible.

"Luna?"

Vincent's voice reaches me through the door, his voice as calm and steady as always. But it feels like a thunderclap in my ears.

I clutch the phone tightly, my heart pounding as I try to pull myself together.

"What?" I manage, my voice sharper than I mean for it to be.

The door cracks open and Vincent's face appears. He scrutinizes me, his expression pinched with concentration.

"Are you alright?"

"Why?"

The corner of his mouth dips into a frown. "I noticed your car is parked half on the grass out front, and that it's got a scrape all along the side."

I blink. "What?"

"Did you hit something?"

I try to picture the drive home, but I know that even if I didn't have aphantasia, my memory would be blurred. Was it possible that I'd hit some car and just kept on going? I'm normally a good driver, but I suppose it was possible, as panicked and scared as I was.

I push past Vincent, clutching my phone so tightly it feels like it might crack further in my hand. My feet pad against the hardwood as I head for the front door.

Vincent's right behind me, and he asks again, "Are you sure you're alright?"

"I'm fine," I snap over my shoulder, but the word tastes bitter as it leaves my mouth. *Fine?* That's laughable. Fine didn't cover the confession I'd just read, the guilt squeezing my chest, or the fact that my editor was a murderer who might want me dead. Fine was a lie, and judging by the look on Vincent's face, he knew it.

The cold air slams into me as I step outside and glance at my Range Rover.

Vincent wasn't lying.

Next to Vincent's Honda, my car sits at an awkward angle, one wheel crooked on the curb, the others haphazardly on the gravel. The scrape along the side gleams under the porch light, a jagged, metallic wound that stands out against the glossy black paint. It's fresh, glaring, undeniable.

I grimace and step closer, ignoring the discomfort in my feet as they press against the gravel. I run my fingers all along the damage. The paint is peeled back, bad enough that I can see the exposed metal beneath.

How had I missed *this*?

Taking in the jagged line, and the way it runs almost the entire length the car, I can't help but wonder what I hit. Another car? A pole? A tree? I'd been too focused on escaping, on putting as much distance between me and Janice's house as possible, to notice anything else.

"You're shaking," Vincent says.

"I'm fine," I say again. But I don't look at him. I can't. It's almost embarrassing, seeing the evidence of how crazed my panic had made me. I press my hands to my temple, trying to massage out the forming headache. It seems like things are piling up, one by one, and it was finally beginning to feel like I was starting to drown.

Vincent rests his hand on my shoulder. "I know someone who can get it fixed up as good as new. Let me take care of it, okay?"

Before I can answer, my phone buzzes in my hand, my loud ringtone startling the both of us. I'm getting a call. I glance at the screen to see who it is, but the fractures spiderwebbing across the glass makes it difficult. Still, I catch enough of the letters to know who it is.

Alyssa Lake.

SEVENTEEN

"Luna Harrow, I'm so glad you answered!"

Alyssa's voice bursts through the phone, sugary and bright, but it grates against my nerves like nails on a chalkboard. I'm not anywhere near as glad as she is, but I know better than to ignore her.

When Alyssa Lake calls, you answer.

"How have you been?" she asks, her tone so casual it's almost mocking.

"Busy," I say, the word coming out clipped, almost curt. I clear my throat, forcing my voice to soften. "Just trying to wrap up this next book for the fans, you know?"

"Ah, is that where you've been hiding?"

Hiding. The word lands like a slap, sharp and stinging. I glance over my shoulder at Vincent, who's still lingering by the porch. I wave him off, letting him know I'll be a minute, and take a few steps away, just far enough that he won't hear everything I'm saying.

"Hiding?" I repeat, feigning ignorance.

"Oh, come now, Luna," she says, her voice dropping

slightly. "It's just the two of us on this call. Let's be honest. You're in trouble because of the controversy, and I know it's eating away at you."

My nails, already chewed to jagged stubs, dig into my palm as I clench my fist. Her words hit too close to home, and I hate how exposed I feel, like she's picked me apart without even trying.

"It's just the two of us?" I ask.

"It's just us," she confirms, and I can hear the smug smile curling her lips through the phone.

"Fine," I answer. "You're right. I haven't loved how fans have drawn on the similarities between *Don't Breathe Twice* and Val's unfortunate tragedy, but that's all they are. Similarities. I'm not worried."

I wonder if she can hear the lie in my words.

"Let me guess, your sales are better than ever, right?"

I don't answer.

She chuckles from the other side of the phone. "I see what you're trying to do. You think that if you churn out books fast enough, then fans will forget about that poor grieving mother and all the trouble she's stirring up. It's not a bad strategy, but I know these readers better than even you. So trust me when I say your plan is not going to work here."

Her words drip with condescension, and my stomach twists with anger. She's right, of course. That is exactly what I'm trying to do—or at least, it's what *we're* trying to do. Me and my serial killer of an editor.

"And why won't it work?"

"Because, I'm moving forward with a segment on you."

My heart skips a beat. "What?"

"That's right," she says, practically purring now. "You're all anybody's talking about. #LunaHarrowExposed, #LunaHarrow, and #MissMurder are the top three trending topics on all of Momnt. Now, if you ask me, I'd rather move on and explore something new, but just like you, I have to give the fans what they want."

I scoff, the sound bitter and harsh. "I thought you said, 'Let's be honest.'"

She laughs. "Oh, Luna. Honesty is *so* subjective, don't you think?"

I don't respond. I can't. Alyssa Lake is doing a segment. On me.

"Now, the way I look at this, this could be the opportunity you need to clear the air. Every fan of yours will tune in to watch, and they'll know you for who you are."

"You want me on the show," I stumble over the words, surprised.

"Of course I do! I need a guest, and who better than you?" She lets the words hangs for a moment, then chuckles. "Well, there is always Val Felder. But between me and you, I think that you would be the *much* better guest."

"You're milking this, aren't you? All for your own gain."

"You must be joking. I do hate repeating myself. I'm trying to give the fans what they want. And clearly what they want is you, Miss Murder."

"You're a snake," I snarl.

There's a pause, and somehow, I just know she's set

aside whatever other things she was looking at and is giving me her undivided attention.

"A snake? I am nothing but an opportunist. Just like you."

"We're nothing alike."

"Is that so? Then tell me why you haven't issued a simple public statement? Or even made the effort to reach out to Ms. Felder? It might have been enough to settle the fans down, let things get back on as normal. But you didn't bother, because you know what I know. There is opportunity in this, and you know what fans love. A good mystery, and what does a good mystery require?"

I don't respond. I can't.

"Absolute and utter silence."

I remain quiet.

Alyssa chuckles softly, and I get the sense that she's relaxed again. "I told you before, I admire you. I wasn't lying. So, what's it to be, Luna? Will you appear on the segment, or will I have to give Ms. Felder a call?"

I close my eyes and breathe, losing myself in my spiraling thoughts. Whether I liked it or not, things would come to a head soon.

"Luna?" Alyssa's voice breaks through to me.

"I'll do it."

I feel her smile again. "Good. I'll let you know once I have a date confirmed. And if you don't mind, stay quiet until we get you on air. Like I said, the fans love the mystery."

"What's the segment called?"

"The Truth About Miss Murder," she answers. I hear a voice in the background. Alyssa muttered a response. A moment later, she comes back to the phone. "Anyway, I have to go now. I'll see you soon!"

The line clicks, the silence rushing in as I lower the phone with a shaking hand.

"Luna?" Vincent's voice startles me. I had forgotten he was here. "Everything okay?"

"It's fine."

Fine. I'm beginning to hate that word.

He gestures toward the Range Rover. "Your car. Are you... fine with me getting it taken to the shop?"

"No, not yet," I say. With so much control getting wrestled away from me, I wasn't willing to lose control over being able to drive myself somewhere. Whatever needed doing to the car could wait until after all this had been dealt with.

"Are you sure? I'm not sure your car is exactly safe to drive."

"I'm sure," I say, waving him off, not caring as I head inside. But the moment I step through the doorway, something feels... wrong. It's subtle at first, a shift in the air I can't quite place. I pause, scanning the space, my eyes skimming over the couch, the table, the shoes by the door.

That's when I remember.

Stephen's stuff is gone, because I'd thrown it out. Every trace of him is gone, and a new kind of dread grips me, tightening like a vice around my chest. How had it not occurred to me until now? If Stephen was having an affair with Janice, then he was in danger. Real, tangible danger. I hated him for what he'd done—how could I not?

But no matter how much I despised his betrayal, he didn't deserve to die for it.

I pull my phone from my pocket, and the cracked screen stares back at me. I try to unlock it, but the fractures make it nearly impossible to press the right buttons.

"Vincent!" I shout, my voice trembling with urgency.

He appears in the doorway almost immediately, "Yes?"

"Can I borrow your phone?" I ask, holding out my hand. "I need to call Stephen."

Confusion ripples across his features. "Stephen?"

"Yes, Stephen!" I snap, my panic bleeding into my tone. "Please, just—quickly!"

Vincent reaches into his pocket without another word and hands me his phone. My fingers tremble as I take it, dialing Stephen's number as quickly as I can. I press the phone to my ear, every muscle in my body tensed as I wait.

It rings once. Then twice. My pulse hammers against my ribs, the sound of the ringback tone stretching endlessly in my ears.

Voicemail.

I pull the phone away, staring at the screen like it might change if I try again. I redial, pressing the phone to my ear. It rings once, then goes silent, the robotic voice telling me to leave a message.

"No, no, no," I mutter, dialing again, my thumb hitting the button harder than necessary. The same result.

Would I receive another brown envelope soon? Would Janice hand me another manuscript, this one written on the murder of a cheater? Would Stephen's body be lying cold somewhere, the victim of my editor's twisted sense of storytelling?

Vincent's voice pulls me back. "I checked for his things," he says softly, his tone almost hesitant.

"What?" I whirl on him, my mind still spinning from the unanswered calls.

"I got rid of Stephen's things. The stuff left over," he says. He pauses, then adds, "Should I not have?"

The words catch me off guard, knocking the wind out of my already ragged breath. My mind stumbles, torn between the fear clawing at my chest and the weight of what he's just said.

"No," I manage after a beat, the word tumbling out unsteady. "I mean... yes. I don't know." My grip on the phone tightens. "Why did you...?"

"You told me you need his stuff gone," Vincent says.

My chest tightens, a strange mix of gratitude and something else I can't name swirling in my stomach. I swallow hard, my thoughts still fixated on Stephen's unanswered phone.

"It's fine," I say, though my voice is far from convincing. That damn word again. "It's just..."

"You're worried," Vincent finishes for me. "About Stephen."

I nod, my throat too tight to form words.

He doesn't press further, just gestures toward the phone in my hand. "Try again. If you can't reach him tonight, you'll figure out what to do in the morning. You always do."

His calm certainty should be reassuring, but it isn't. Not this time. Not when Stephen could already be dead.

I try calling Stephen another three times, but he doesn't pick up. Vincent gives me an apologetic look as he takes the phone back, promising that he'd let me know the moment that Stephen called him back.

I contemplate sending Janice a message through Momnt, demanding to know whether or not she's done something to him. But I don't. I don't want to even put the thought into her head, because I'm not sure what I would do if I knew that I was the reason for his murder.

Instead, I settle myself onto the couch and snack, stress eating and watching more trash TV while I desperately check my phone every two minutes. I prepare myself for yet another long sleepless night when I finally hear the sound of a notification.

I snatch my phone up. The text message is from Stephen. I breathe a sharp sigh of relief and jab at my broken screen, trying not to get frustrated as I attempt to open the message. Eventually it does, and though it's near impossible to read it, just enough letters make it through for me to understand what he's saying.

You said you were done with me, right? So stop calling me. I'm moving on from this place.

Before I can even attempt to reply with my broken phone, I see a line appear at the bottom of the chat.

Stephen has blocked you.

Moving on from this place? I frown. What does that even mean? Was he seriously blocking me and moving somewhere else, just because we broke up? What about Janice?

Wait... this was a good thing. If Stephen was planning on moving, then he'd be safe from her, and despite the fact that he was a good-for-nothing dirtbag, that's all I wanted for him. I laugh as a weight lifts itself from my shoulder.

Footsteps echo behind me and I look back. It's Vincent. He rounds the couch and sits next to me, reaching for one of the chips.

"Did he get back to you?" Vincent asks.

The chip crunches in his mouth as he watches the show with me.

"He did. Everything's fine. Sorry about freaking out."

The corner of his mouth lifts, "You've been stressed lately. You have a lot going on."

"That's one way to put it," I mutter.

I crunch another chip between my teeth, the salt stinging my tongue. The trashy reality show blares in the background, but my mind is only half-focused on the drama onscreen. Vincent sits beside me, calm as always, his presence steady in a way that makes me feel less like I'm drowning.

"How's my mom doing?" I ask suddenly, breaking the silence. My voice comes out softer than I intended.

"She's resting," he answers. "Everything's stable. Machines are running fine."

I nod, the tension in my chest easing just a little. "That's good," I murmur, fiddling with a corner of the chip bag. "I don't check on her as much as I should."

"You've got a lot on your plate, and she knows that," Vincent replies, his tone even. "But she's in good hands."

I glance over at him, and for a moment, the faint buzz

of the TV fades into the background. He doesn't just say it—he means it. He's here for her, for me, even when everything else feels like it's falling apart.

"Vincent," I start, hesitating for a moment. "What are you doing for dinner?"

He looks at me, surprised, as if the question catches him off guard. "Dinner? You mean this isn't it?"

"No," I laugh. I clear my throat, trying to sound casual. "You've been stepping up a lot lately, and I've been... well, not great company. I figured the least I could do is make sure you're fed a real meal."

The corner of his mouth quirks into a small smile, and he leans back slightly, his gaze steady. "You don't have to do that."

"I know," I say, meeting his eyes. "But I want to."

He watches me for a moment, his expression softening. "Alright," he says finally. "I'm in."

"Good," I reply, brushing crumbs off my hands and standing up. "I'm not promising anything gourmet, though."

He chuckles. "As long as it's not burnt, I'll take it."

We go to the kitchen and I pull open the fridge, rummaging through its contents, trying to figure out what I can throw together.

"I'll chop," he offers, stepping forward and grabbing a cutting board before I can protest. "What's on the menu?"

"I was thinking pasta. Maybe a salad, if we have enough lettuce that hasn't gone bad."

"Pasta it is," he says, rolling up his sleeves. His movements are easy, like it's as natural for him to do this as it is for him to adjust my mother's equipment. I let myself relax into the simplicity of it, allowing for everything else to fade away—two people making dinner, no drama, no phone calls, no looming catastrophes.

We move around the kitchen in sync, the silence broken only by the sound of boiling water and the rhythmic chop of Vincent's knife against the cutting board. It's... nice. Easy, even. A strange reprieve from everything that's going on.

When everything is ready, we sit across from each other at the small table. The food is simple but comforting, and for the first time in what feels like days, I don't feel like I'm holding my breath.

"Thanks for this," I say, breaking the quiet as I twirl pasta around my fork. "I needed the distraction."

Vincent nods, his gaze steady. "You're welcome."

For a while, we just eat. I let myself forget about the controversy, about Janice, about Alyssa Lake and her segment. It's just Vincent and me, and the soft, gentle hum of the house around us.

But as I glance up at him, catching the faint smile tugging at the corner of his mouth, I can't help but think that maybe there's something here, between us.

The question is... will it still be here after everything comes crashing down?

EIGHTEEN

My fingers drum on the desk as I wait impatiently for the technician to see if he can fix my phone. It's been over thirty minutes—long enough for me to have browsed every display in the store and conveniently noted all the shiny, overpriced new phone models they're pushing this year. But me? I'm happy enough with my three-year-old iPhone. It's not like much has changed.

"Well?" I prompt, eyeing the technician again as he pokes at my shattered screen with a tool that looks more suited to fixing jewelry than electronics.

He looks up, grimacing like he's about to tell me the worst news of my life. "Sorry, Ms. Harrow. Based on what I can see, there's damage to the interior components of the phone, as well as the screen. We can fix it, of course, but well..."

"Let me guess." I cross my arms. "It'll be more expensive than just getting onto a new phone contract."

"Exactly that." He nods quickly, his tone almost relieved that I've figured it out for him. "You could even walk out of here today with a brand-new phone. I can help transfer your data, too."

I sigh, disappointed but not surprised. Somehow, I just knew walking into this store that I'd leave feeling scammed. That's how it always is.

"I liked my phone," I mutter, more to myself than to him.

He blinks at me, like the concept of wanting to hold onto an older phone is utterly alien in this day and age.

"Fine," I relent. "Just get me whatever phone makes the most sense. I'd like to be out of here in the next hour—I have a busy day."

"Absolutely!" he chirps, suddenly energized, as if I've made his whole week. Before I can say anything else, he's up and pulling the latest iPhone model off the shelf, stacking it with a screen protector, a case, and every other accessory I didn't bother with last time.

When he sits back down, I see that he's chosen the most expensive version of the model. Of course he has. But honestly, I couldn't care less at this point. My mind's already somewhere else.

Stick to our routine. Don't question the process.

Janice's message replays in my head, every word a warning I can't shake. Did she seriously think I could trust her after everything? After I'd pieced together what she was capable of? She was a serial killer—and a cheat.

As long as she was around, everything I'd built was at risk. My career. My mother. My life. Alyssa Lake sniffing around was just another reminder that it was only a matter of time before someone connected the dots. I had a gut feeling about that. And Alyssa, of all people, would take that truth and broadcast it to the world.

But how do I stop it?

I can't go to Val Felder. She'd never back down—not when she's fighting for justice for her son. Anything I say to her would probably just fuel her fire.

I can't just stand by and do nothing, either. Doing nothing means letting Janice control my fate, and there's no reality where I'm okay with that. With the bitter taste of her and Stephen's betrayal still in my mouth, I know that neither me nor my ego could stomach the thought of having her control Miss Murder.

Going to the police feels like the nuclear option. It would destroy me. They'd slap cuffs on me before I even finished explaining, my brand would evaporate, and the world would happily replace me with another author who could serve up their fix of murder and suspense. And what would happen to my mother then?

I lean back in the chair, closing my eyes as a dull headache begins to form behind them.

"Thinking about your next book?" the technician asks, his voice cutting through my thoughts.

"What?" I blink, startled. My mind stumbles to catch up, surprised that he recognizes me. Don't know why, though. There's probably more people that'd know my face than ever. After all, it's being blasted across the most popular social media apps.

"Your next book," he repeats, glancing up from the phone he's setting up for me. "You had that look—like you were working through something in your head."

"Oh." I force a half-smile, brushing off the question. I

hope that he's not going to ask about the controversy. "Yeah, something like that."

"I'm a fan, by the way," he says, his tone casual, like he's mentioning the weather. "Your thrillers are great. *Don't Breathe Twice*? Had me up all night."

I stare at him, caught completely off guard. "You... liked that book?"

"Of course." He grins. "It's one of my favorites. I know my girlfriend would never admit it, on account of all the... you know, but I know it's hers too."

"That's..." I trail off, unsure how to respond. "Thank you."

He shrugs, his hands moving deftly as he works on my new phone. "So, are the murders real?"

The question stops me cold. My pulse stutters as I meet his gaze, expecting to see suspicion or accusation. But there's none. He's just... curious.

It's foolish, I know it is, but I'm feeling more brazen than ever. Maybe it's because I know that inside of the next week, everything I have could be lost.

"Yes."

His brows lift slightly, but there's no shock. No judgment. He just nods, like I've told him something as mundane as the weather forecast.

"Cool," he says simply.

I blink. "Cool?"

"Yeah." He shrugs, his focus already back on the phone. "People profit off murder all the time. Netflix, true-crime podcasts, news stations. It's not like you actually murdered anyone, right?"

The way he says it, so casual, so matter-of-fact, leaves me momentarily speechless. "No," I manage. "I didn't."

Janice did.

"Here you go," he says, handing the phone back to me with a faint smile. "You're all set."

The phone's screen lights up, pristine and new, and my fingers hover over it as I try to process what just happened. He says something, and I completely miss it until I look up and realize he's staring at me, waiting for a response.

"I'm sorry, can you repeat that?" I ask.

"I know you just came out with *The Broken Boy*, but when do you think your next book is coming?"

At first thought, it's a bit of a silly question to ask. After all, I'd been known for releasing a best seller on the first of every month for over the last two years. But then I start to see things from his perspective. He must know just from the look on my face that I'm struggling with the controversy. I start to catch onto his deeper question, and it's not *when* I'll release something new, but *if* I will.

"Soon," I say, knowing that wasn't much of an answer. But it seems to keep him satisfied enough as his face glows up with an ear-to-ear grin.

"Can't wait to get my hands on it. Have a great day," he says, before conspicuously looking around, leaning in, and continuing, "Miss Murder."

I nod, mumbling something that might vaguely resemble a "thanks," and head for the door.

Once I'm back in my car, I open the Momnt app. It's been days since I checked it, and with #MissMurder, #LunaHarrow, and #LunaHarrowExposed all still trending, I'm not surprised when my notifications are maxed out.

Many of them are from fans begging me to make a public statement. I scroll deeper to see what else they've been saying. To my surprise—and mild relief—it seems like a good portion of people have accepted my silence as a deliberate strategy. Even Val Felder, who's usually fanning the flames, hasn't posted anything new. Maybe that's because she didn't really care to control the narrative, other than to put me in the spotlight for the supposedly horrible crime that I committed.

If only they knew the truth.

Instead, the conversation has shifted. They're not demanding an explanation—they're speculating. Wondering. Their posts are circling around what's going to happen to me, what I'm going to do, and what *they* would do if they were in my position. But none of them could really know my position, or just how trapped I am.

I land on a video of a teenager sitting in front of a cluttered bookshelf, my books prominently displayed behind her. The title below the video reads: *Are Miss Murder's Thrillers Based on Real Murders?*

The girl adjusts her glasses, and with the smug confidence of Sherlock Holmes, she leans into the camera.

"We all know about Miss Murder and *Don't Breathe Twice*, how it sounds exactly like the Felder case. But what if it's not a one-off coincidence?"

She reaches back and pulls one of my books from the shelf and holds it up to the camera. It's *Whisper No More*. My mouth goes dry.

"Let's take a look at this one. I'll bet you didn't know

that there was an unsolved murder in a town called Whitmore, where a young woman was brutally strangled in a library. Sound familiar?"

My pulse spikes, until she puts the book aside and starts to ramble off the most ridiculous of theories, strung together by connections that were weak at best. The comments seem to be eating it up though.

I grimace, because if even a handful of people dig deeper and find the patterns, it won't take long for them to uncover the truth. And once that happens...

I shake my head, trying to push the thought away. I need to shut this down. I need to figure out a way to—

A notification pops up, drawing my attention. It's from Alyssa Lake's official account.

My breath catches as I tap it, my dread sinking deeper when I see the post she's shared: a slickly produced teaser video for an upcoming segment.

The screen is dark at first, a haunting piano melody playing in the background. Then my face appears—black-and-white, shadowed, and deliberately unflattering. Beneath it, the title reads: *The Truth About Miss Murder*.

Her voice cuts through, polished and professional, just as always. "Miss Murder, resting at the heart of the biggest controversy to ever strike the book community. But soon you will have the truth, straight from the lips of Luna Harrow herself."

Clips of my old interviews flash across the screen, my smiling face juxtaposed with eerie headlines and crime scene photos. The teaser ends with Alyssa herself, staring directly into the camera, her signature smirk tugging at her lips.

"Follow me to be the first to hear the announcement of when we will go live to discuss the controversy surrounding her books, Val Felder, and the questions everyone's been asking."

The screen fades to black, replaced by the hashtags already trending: #TheTruthAboutMissMurder and #LunaHarrowExposed.

I sit there, staring at my phone, my breath shallow and uneven. The teaser is everywhere—shared, reposted, dissected. Alyssa's marketing machine is already in full swing, building hype for the segment that could destroy me.

I toss my phone into the passenger seat and rest my head against the steering wheel, banging it softly against the leather. I needed a *plan*, because like it not, all of this was closing in on me. But before I can contemplate any further, my phone starts to ring.

It's an unknown number.

With a frown, I slowly reach for it and hold it up to my ear.

"Hello?"

"Is this Luna Harrow?" A male voice asks in a deep, serious tone.

A shiver runs down my spine. "Yes?"

"My name is Detective Hardy. Do you have a minute?"

NINETEEN

I hang up before he can say a word. Before I can say anything that'll dig me a hole so deep I'll never climb out of it.

But the sound of my ringtone plays through the car. It's the detective again. He knows I've hung up on him. When the ringtone stops, I see the notification on my phone that there's been a voicemail left for me.

I should be afraid. My heart should be pounding against my ribs, with sweat clinging to the back of my neck. But the kind of fear I should feel right now—the panic, the adrenaline—isn't there. Instead, all I feel is a crushing numbness, wrapping itself around me like a heavy, suffocating blanket.

The cops. Of all the people who could've called, it had to be them. That fact should terrify me. But it doesn't. It leaves me hollow, my hands steady as I turn over the engine and pull out onto the road.

The numbness clings to me as I drive, the steady hum of traffic around me blending into white noise. For a while, it feels like enough. Like maybe, if I stay wrapped in this emptiness, I won't have to face what's waiting for me on the other side of it.

But it doesn't last. Eventually, reality pushes its way in, pouring over me like ice water. And with it comes the suffocating realization: there's no escaping this nightmare. No fixing it, no rewinding time, no magic loophole that will save me. I can see that clearly now.

The traffic flows around me, and my grip on the steering wheel tightens as my thoughts shift, settling on the one thing that still matters. The one thing this has always been about.

My mother.

She's all that matters now. Not my career, not the controversy, not the tens of thousands of voices tearing me apart online. Just her. Because if the truth comes out and the dots get connected, there's a prison cell waiting for me. A numbered orange jumpsuit. A locked door slamming shut behind me. And that means there will be no one left to care for her, except for Vincent. But I'm not foolish enough to think that he'd stay out of his own good will. He had his own life to live, his own money he'd need to earn. He wasn't going to stay either.

The thought hits like a punch to the gut, knocking the air out of me. My chest tightens as those all too familiar words slip into my mind.

You'll never write anything real.

The worst part about it all? My old teacher was right. I never did. Every book, every word, every accolade—they weren't real. They weren't mine. They were *hers*.

And now, I'm going to suffer the consequences of that.

I blink, my vision blurring slightly as I replay the steps that led me here. If I had just figured it out earlier—if I had committed myself to figuring out how to get over my aphantasia and actually writing a book before I published *Don't Breathe Twice*—then maybe none of this would have happened.

Maybe Val Felder would have never known my name. Maybe Alyssa Lake wouldn't be preparing to ruin me on live television. Maybe there wouldn't be cops dialing my number, looking for answers I don't know how to give.

But I didn't. I took the easy way out.

It's not long before I reach the house and turn into the driveway, my tires crunching over the gravel. I switch the engine off and sit there for a while, staring at this great big, beautiful house of mine that'll soon be taken from me.

The sun starts to dip toward the horizon, and with a heavy sigh, I get out and go inside. The soft, steady sounds of my mother's equipment draw me into her room.

I lean against the doorway, resting my head against the doorframe. She's sleeping. Her breathing is calm, her face is relaxed, and for a moment, it feels like she's not suffering. It feels like I'm a teenager again, and I've just snuck back into the house to find her sleeping.

"I love you, mom," I whisper.

Soft footsteps sound behind me. It's Vincent.

"Hey," he says in a soft voice.

"Hey."

He hears my voice and tilts his head, catching the note of... what? Depression? Dismay? I'm not even sure anymore.

I nod toward my mother. "How is she?"

He hesitates, his eyes still studying me like he's trying to figure me out. In the end, though, he sighs and answers, "Today was a good day."

"Good."

"Did you manage to get your phone fixed?"

"Not exactly," I say as I lift it enough for him to see that it was a brand new phone. The voicemail notification stares at me. I think Vincent's seen it, but he doesn't make a mention of it.

"Looks like they got you with the new contract deal, huh?"

I grimace and nod.

For a while, we stay there and watch my sleeping mother, listening to the sound of her machines droning and beeping. I know Vincent has other things he'd probably like to be doing, like catching up on a book or getting ready to go running. It was getting dark, after all. But for some reason, he stays, like he can sense that I'm in need of his company.

I hate to admit that I do. When Stephen was here, I'd gotten used to feeling not so alone. Now that he's gone, I'm starting to remember how awful it feels.

My phone buzzes in my hand, gently reminding me to check my voicemails. Vincent glances down at my phone. I know he's seen the notification on the screen.

I turn away from my mother's room, and motioning

for him to follow me, I go back to the living room. He sits across from me on the couch and waits to hear whatever I'm concerned about.

I bite my lips, trying to figure out how much I can tell him. He's trustworthy, capable of keeping my secrets, or at least, *some* of them anyways. I know that much. But still, there's a professional line between us that shouldn't be crossed, and I shouldn't be dragging him into my problems.

Taking a deep breath, I look up at him and ask, "Vincent, how much do you know about the controversy going on about Miss Murder?"

I wait for his face to scrunch up in confusion, but his face remains stoic. I blink and lean forward, "Wait, do you already know?"

"I do have Momnt, Luna."

"Why didn't you ever say anything?"

He shrugs and leans back into the couch, interlacing his hands over his chest. "Because none of it matters to me. I know what kind of person you are, and that's enough."

The chill that's gripped my heart melts in the warmth spreading through my body. A smile splits my face, but it only lasts a moment. I lift up my phone. "Well, it seems to matter to some people. Like the cops."

Concern flashes through his eyes, and I can tell that things are different now. Now, he's worried.

"What did they say?"

"I don't know. I hung up before he could say anything. But he left a voicemail."

He grimaces, and perhaps understandably so. I don't

think you're supposed to hang up on the police. I draw a deep breath. His eyes catch onto mine.

"Want to listen to the voicemail together?" he asks.

Inside, I breathe a sigh of relief. It's nice to not have to deal with the cops myself. Funny, how something like this can come along and make you feel like you're suddenly *not* an adult. Like you should be calling for your mom to come help. But my mother wasn't well, so Vincent was as good as it was going to get.

A few moments later, the detective's voice comes through the phone.

"Hi, Ms. Harrow, this is Detective Hardy. It seems that the call... dropped after I introduced myself, so I'm leaving you a message. In an attempt to keep this out of the public eye, please call me back as soon as possible to discuss a... *concerning* incident that has occurred." He leaves his number, then the phone clicks.

My eyes raise to meet Vincent's.

"Are you wanting to call him back?" he asks.

There's a moment of hesitation from me. I'd decided on the way home that this was really the only path forward for me, especially if I want my mother to have even a remote chance of coming out of it okay. Maybe if I came forward about Janice being a serial killer, I could negotiate some sort of deal that would allow for my mother to have some sort of special care, using some of the funds I'd 'earned', on account of me going to prison. But despite that internal decision, it's hard for me to even say anything out loud.

"Don't." His voice is firm, and there's concern and worry in his eyes. He sits closer to me on the couch, resting his hand over mine. "You shouldn't speak to them."

"You don't know what I've done," I say, my chin starting to quiver.

"I know that you're a good person."

His words make my eyes well up with tears. I *am* a good person. Just an unfortunate one, too.

"The police don't have any reasons to go after you," he continues. But he doesn't know. They have over twenty books' worth of reasons to come after me. "I don't know anybody who's been implicated over rumors on social media. But I do know people who have gotten themselves into trouble."

I know what he's saying. It was entirely possible that the police don't know to the extent of just how bad things were. They could be focused on just *one* book's worth of suspicion. Not more than twenty.

I open my mouth to object, but he shakes his head.

"Luna, think about it. Why are they *calling* you?"

Now, I hesitate. It was a good question. If they seriously believed that they were onto the trail of a murderer, particularly one that was famous, then I'd be hearing a knock at the door.

He sees that I'm starting to work it out and gives me a soft smile.

"I'm not sure what it is that they want, but I don't think you should give it to them."

"Why?"

"Because at the end of the day, this is their job, and I don't think they're looking out for Luna Harrow as much as they are themselves."

He has a point there. I breathe out. "Alright."

His hand lingers on mine, and for some reason, I can't pull my eyes away from the warmth of his. Then one of the machines from my mother's room suddenly emits a loud beep, shattering the moment between us.

Vincent swears under his breath and gives me an apologetic smile as he gets to his feet. I can tell he wants to stay, but he knows he needs to go help her.

"Go," I say. "I'll be fine."

"Are you sure?"

"Yes," I say.

Vincent gives me one last smile before he turns and disappears back down the hall.

When he's gone, I bury my face in my hands and let out a soft groan. I lied to him. I don't feel fine. Vincent has kept me from taking the easy way out by calling Detective Hardy back. But I know that he is right. Why give the cops enough rope to hang myself when all they have to go off of is the rumor mill of Momnt?

Well, they probably have enough suspicious cause to pull me in based on the similarities between *Don't Breathe Twice* and the murder of Val Felder's son, but if that were true, then they'd be on my doorstep like Vincent said.

Besides, was it even illegal to write books on the details of real crime scenes? I'm not so sure, but it could be argued in court, right? I should probably have a lawyer look into it.

With the weight of everything suddenly back on my shoulders, I know that I have to figure out a way through this. And soon, because like it or not, Alyssa Lake's going to go forward with that segment and I had to have an answer for both her and the fans.

The sound of a notification pulls my attention back to my phone. There's a text waiting for me.

And it's from Janice.

TWENTY

With a shaking hand, I open her text.

Is Stephen with you?

My eyes narrow and my face flushes red with anger. Stephen? Is she trying to taunt me, to throw him in my face?

You know he's not, Janice. Why are you texting me?

Her response comes quickly, as if she'd been waiting for my reply.

We need to meet. Tomorrow. Not at our usual spot.

I blink at the screen, the words blurring slightly as my grip tightens on the phone. Not at our usual spot. My stomach churns. Janice is meticulous, almost obsessively so. She thrives on routine, on predictability. For her to break that pattern means one of two things: either she's spiraling because of Alyssa Lake's teaser, or she's planning something.

I type back slowly, choosing my words carefully.

Why?

The dots appear, pausing longer than usual before her reply comes through.

We need to talk. Face to face.

About what? I ask.

You know what.

A chill runs through me, and for a moment, I consider ignoring her. But deep down, I know this conversation has been inevitable ever since I found out about her and Stephen's affair, and about her being my mystery Charles Dickens. I've been avoiding it for too long, and now it's here, staring me in the face, demanding my attention.

Where?

She sends an address. Somewhere downtown, a diner I vaguely remember from years ago, tucked away on a quiet street. It's far enough out of the way to be discreet but public enough to feel somewhat safe.

I stare at the screen for a long moment, my thumb hovering over the keyboard. I know I should say no, demand to know why she's breaking routine, why she suddenly wants to meet somewhere else. But I don't. Instead, I type two words and hit send before I can second-guess myself.

I'll come.

With any luck, this meeting with Janice will give me some idea of how to escape this mess. Maybe I can turn things back on her—get her to give herself up to Detective Hardy and set me free.

After all, what was it she said?

I did it for you.

If she really cared for me as much as she claimed, wouldn't she be willing to quietly turn herself in? Take the fall and let me walk away unscathed? It's not like I asked her to kill anyone. She made that choice, not me.

Of course, if she did that, it would also mean the end of Miss Murder. People would figure it out eventually—that my editor, not me, was the *true* Miss Murder behind the books. My brand would crumble, my fans would turn away, and the world would finally see me for what I am: a fraud.

Still, if it meant staying out of a jail cell, wasn't it worth it? I could walk away, alive and free, with enough money to keep my mother cared for. That's what matters, isn't it?

But even as I try to convince myself, the thought sits bitterly in my chest. I'd be alive, yes. But free? Free of Janice, maybe. Free of prison bars. But free of this shame, this guilt, this constant shadow of failure?

I don't think so.

I would love nothing more than to keep my career and my mother. To have both. But at the end of the day, one matters more than the other. It always has.

Tears well up in my eyes, hot and stinging, and I blink them away furiously. Frustrated, I toss my phone aside and grab the remote, flipping on the TV.

There's not much on, though. Just as I'm about to go to bed, Vincent returns and takes a seat next to me. His sleeves are rolled up, his dark hair slightly tousled, and there's a faint line of worry etched between his eyes.

"Feeling better about everything?" he asks.

I nod, forcing a weak smile. "Just... tired. I'll probably head to bed soon."

"Okay." He pauses, studying me for a moment. "Do you need anything from me?"

I look into his eyes, and a different thought pops into my mind. It occurs to me that we're the only two in this house, besides my mother. My mouth is dry, but I cannot deny the allure of losing myself in his arms and escaping from all of *this*, even if only for a short while.

Except I know that the fallout of that would be so much worse than everything else, because in the end, there would be nobody to care for my mother.

Reluctantly, I shake my head and rise from the couch, already retreating toward the hall that would take me to my bedroom. Alone. "No, I'm good. Thanks, Vincent."

I pause and glance back at him, hesitating. "Oh, by the way... I'll probably be out all day tomorrow, and I know we're short on groceries. Feel free to order food in, if you like. My treat."

"Where are you headed?"

"I'm meeting Janice tomorrow."

His eyelids flicker upward in surprise. "Janice? That's your editor, right?"

"Yeah," I sigh. "It is."

"You already have another book ready?"

"No, she texted me to see if I could meet her at some diner downtown. Probably to talk about the controversy or..." I trail off, waving a hand vaguely. "Something."

"Sounds... not fun."

I grunt.

"What diner?"

I glance down at my phone. "Some place called JoJo's?"

"Yeah, I know it. It's alright." He pauses, like he wants to say something else.

"What is it?"

He swallows and looks up at me from the couch, his expression softening. "Don't suppose that you would ever like to go there with me?"

I'm left a little breathless. Vincent wants to take me out? I'm reminded again of how alone we are, and I so desperately want to stay awake with him. But I know in my heart that there's really not any place for him until I've fixed everything.

"I'd like that, but..." I trail off again.

"You have a lot going on," he says.

A breath escapes me. "Yes. *So* much going on."

He smiles, its genuineness freeing me from the worry of letting him down too. "Don't worry. I can wait."

"Please do," I say, biting my lip and half turning away. I pause, temptation pulling at me again, but this time, I do the smart thing. "Goodnight, Vincent."

"Goodnight, Luna."

TWENTY-ONE

The coffee at JoJo's is terrible.

I'm sitting in a cracked vinyl booth, the mug in front of me steaming faintly. I haven't taken more than a sip, but the taste still lingers—bitter and burnt, like it's been sitting in the pot all day. The din of the diner buzzes around me: plates clattering, silverware scraping, the low hum of a radio playing an old country song. It's all background noise, muted by the tension in my chest as I glance at the clock on my phone for the third time.

Janice is late.

I shift uncomfortably, brushing imaginary crumbs from the table as I try not to think about all the ways this meeting could go wrong. It's already wrong. This isn't our usual spot, and Janice doesn't do "not usual." She's a creature of habit, of meticulous planning and carefully constructed routines. For her to deviate from that feels like a deliberate choice, one meant to keep me off balance.

Or maybe it's just her toying with me again. Her way of reminding me that she's in control.

I take another glance at the door, half-expecting her to walk in at any moment, her calm demeanor masking whatever game she's playing this time. But it doesn't budge. Just a waitress stepping out from the kitchen, balancing a tray of burgers and fries. I see her eyes flick toward me, like she's wondering how long I'll sit here waiting before I order food.

I check my phone. No new texts. No missed calls. Nothing.

But the minutes tick by, and she still doesn't show.

I check the clock again. Twenty minutes late now. Janice is never late. She's punctual to a fault, arriving exactly on time, never early, never late. My mind starts to wander.

Did she change her mind? Decide I wasn't worth her time? Or worse, was this some kind of trap? A distraction?

I glance toward the windows, the shadows of the parking lot stretching longer as the evening settles in. The diner feels smaller suddenly, and I'm getting the sensation that I'm being watched.

I check over my shoulder, scanning the faces around me. A couple in the corner, an older man nursing a cup of coffee at the counter, the waitress bustling between tables. No one looks suspicious. No one looks out of place.

And yet, I can't shake the feeling that something is wrong.

I grab my phone, my hands trembling slightly as I dial

Janice's number. The line instantly goes to voicemail. I call her again only to hit voicemail a second time.

Why would she send me a text message to arrange a meeting, only to not show?

I stand and my chair scrapes back. I catch one of the waitress's attention.

"Can I help you, darling?" she asks as she chews on a thick wad of gum. I see her look me over, from head to toe, probably wondering why someone wearing rich black pumps would be wasting her time in a diner like this.

"I'm waiting for someone. A woman with a colored ribbon in her hair?"

She blinks at me. "Okay."

I wait, but she just continues to stare at me.

"Well, have you seen her?"

"No."

I clench my jaw, shaking my head. "You're sure?"

"No."

"What do you mean no?"

"Darling, I'm working here. I don't have a photograph memory. People come in, then they leave. Except for you."

"Photographic memory, you mean."

"Sure."

I let out an exasperated sigh, then force a smile. "Thank you, you've been very helpful."

She doesn't even give me a second look before she continues on to the kitchen. I frown and push her out of my mind, instead focusing on Janice.

Why would she text me, arrange a meeting, and then

disappear? It takes a minute before a terrifying possibility roots itself in my mind.

What if this wasn't breaking her routine? What if she arranged it here, at JoJo's, because she never intended to meet me?

The thought darkens.

What if this was all about getting me out of the house?

My stomach drops.

My blood runs cold and I fumble with my phone, pulling up my messages to text Vincent.

Are you at the house? Is everything okay?

The message sends, and I clutch the phone, waiting for a response. But seconds tick by, and there's nothing.

I grab my bag, toss a few bills onto the table, and rush toward the door. The cool evening air hits my face as I step outside, the parking lot empty except for my car. My hands shake as I unlock the door and climb inside, my phone buzzing in my lap.

It's Vincent.

Everything's fine. What's wrong?

Relief floods through me, but it's fleeting, edged with paranoia. I don't know what Janice is doing, but I can't ignore the sinking feeling in my gut.

I text him back, *Has anyone stopped by the house?*

No. You mean Janice? I thought she was meeting you at JoJo's?

I put my phone away without responding and grip the steering wheel tightly. I'll give her ten more minutes, I decide. Ten minutes, and if she doesn't show, I'm done waiting.

But ten minutes pass, and Janice still doesn't show.

I call her again, the phone pressed tight to my ear, but it goes straight to voicemail—just like the last two times. My thumb hovers over the screen for a moment, hesitating, before I text her: Where are you? The message sends, but the dots of her reply never appear. Nothing.

I drop the phone into the cupholder, start the Range Rover, and pull out of the lot. The engine's low rumble fills the silence, but it does nothing to steady the unease crawling beneath my skin. It's a long drive home—nearly an hour, thanks to the traffic—and with every passing second, my anxiety builds.

I punch my foot against the gas pedal, pushing the car above the speed limit and weaving through the traffic. Rationally, I know Vincent texted me that everything's fine. But no matter how hard I try to hold onto that reassurance, it slips through my fingers. The dread pressing down on my chest refuses to budge.

Something is wrong.

The thought burrows deeper as I race down the dark roads, headlights streaking past me. I feel like one of the characters in my books—only I'm not the author anymore. I'm the victim, caught in a killer's sinister web.

When I finally turn into the driveway, my heart sinks. The house is dark, no lights in the windows to greet me. My anxiety spikes as I park haphazardly next to Vincent's car and throw the door open. The slam echoes in the stillness as I sprint toward the front door.

"Vincent?" I call out, my voice shaking as I step inside.

The house is silent, save for the familiar hum and

rhythmic beeps coming from my mother's room. My breathing quickens as I move toward her door, my footsteps echoing in the quiet.

When I flip on the light, my heart jumps to my throat.

She's awake.

Her eyes are open, staring blankly at the ceiling, but her expression is calm. Relief floods through me, my hand pressing against my chest as I force my breathing to slow. She doesn't need to see me like this—panicked and unraveling. I need to be steady, for her.

"Hi, Mom," I say softly, my voice shaky but warm. "How are you?"

I go to her and run my hand over her hair, pressing a kiss against her forehead. Then I look into her eyes and pause. There's a look in them that I've never seen. It's hard to distinguish, but it almost looks like... fear?

"Mom?" I ask. "Everything okay?"

More than ever, I wish she could talk back to me. I search her face for answers, but she only blinks, her eyes still locked on mine. My gaze shifts to the room, scanning every corner, every shadow, trying to figure out what might have scared her. But there's nothing. No sound. No movement.

I turn back toward the hallway, my voice trembling. "Vincent?"

No response.

"Janice?" I call, the name feeling foreign on my tongue, like it doesn't belong here. In my house.

Silence. The kind that seeps into your bones and makes you feel like you're being swallowed whole.

I glance back at my mother. That look in her eyes tightens in my chest. My breaths come shallow and quick as worry coils inside me.

Did Janice do something to Vincent?

The thought is absurd... isn't it? But then, how many murders have I read from her perspective? She's capable of anything. Slaughtering a young child. A full-grown man. Hell, probably me too, if she thought I was in her way.

I pat my mother's shoulder, my hand lingering for a moment longer than necessary. "I'll be back, okay?" My voice wavers, and for a split second, I think I hear something—a whimper, faint and soft. But no. That's impossible. She can't make a sound. Locked-In Syndrome has robbed her of that ability. I misheard, that was all.

I force myself to leave her, stepping out into the hallway and flicking on every light as I move through the house. My footsteps echo faintly.

"Vincent?" I call again, louder this time.

Nothing.

I check the living room, the kitchen, even the guest bathroom. But each one is empty, unbothered without so much as a trace of her. By the time I reach my office at the end of the hall, my heart is pounding in my chest, my nerves starting to stretch thin.

And then I see it.

There's something on my desk.

I pause, my breath catching as my eyes lock onto the object. A brown envelope, resting neatly in the center of the desk like it belongs there. My brow furrows. I thought I'd put the last manuscript away. Unless...

No. This can't be a new one. Can it?

My legs feel heavy as I cross the room to pick it up. The envelope is lighter than the others, and is nowhere near as thick. I know this one isn't the same as before, but I try to convince myself that it is, because the alternative could mean that Janice *was* inside my house.

I drag my finger through the flap and open the envelope, pulling out the manuscript. It's only a handful of pages, enough to publish as a short story, but not much else. There's no convincing myself anymore. Especially as I read the first line.

It had been too easy, this one.

The words blur as my vision tunnels, my heart pounding so hard it feels like my ribs might crack. My fingers grip the edges of the manuscript, the paper trembling in my hands. I force myself to keep reading, even though every fiber of my being screams at me to stop.

I thought that he would be a challenge. That kind, charming Simon had an edge to him. I was excited to hunt him. But it turns out he was filled with the same as all the others. Crimson strokes of nothing.

My stomach twists. Somehow, I know that the dead man's name isn't Simon at all. And the more I read, the more dread starts to seep into my bones.

Simon. Stephen.

The names blur together in my head. My breath quickens as I scan the next line, my fingers clutching the pages so tightly that they crumple at the edges.

He tried to run, of course. They always do. But it didn't matter. The alley narrowed, the walls closing in around him, and when he tripped—oh, that is always my favorite part. The way they scramble, clawing at the ground like they can outrun fate.

I can't breathe. I don't want to keep going. I don't want to see where this is heading, but I can't stop. The words drag me forward.

He begged. Said I would regret this, and that I would be found out. But they all think they're special, don't they? They think that their lies are somehow justifiable. That their betrayals don't count.

Betrayal... Janice must have found out that Stephen was leaving her, that he was moving away. A sob catches in my throat. It's Stephen. It has to be.

He thought he was clever, playing detective. But cleverness doesn't matter when you're caught in my web.

The manuscript slips from my hands, fluttering to the floor like dead leaves. My stomach churns, bile rising in my throat. Playing detective. He wasn't meeting Janice for an affair. He wasn't betraying me.

He was investigating her.

My head spins as I try to piece it together. And while many of those pieces don't fit in a way I can understand, it's clear that he must have suspected her. Maybe he saw the controversy and thought he could help. Maybe, when I broke up with him, he went to her to stop her.

Why? To protect me? To spare me the guilt of destroying my own career and the income I needed to provide for my mother? Or was he just trying to be the hero, thinking he could fix everything on his own?

It doesn't matter now. He's gone.

The room feels smaller, like the walls are closing in. I

press my hands to my face, trying to hold myself together. But through the cracks of my fingers, I see something.

There's a note to the side of the manuscript. A *written* one, with strangely familiar letters.

Miss Murder always gets her ending.

Footsteps echo in the hallway and I jump, my eyes wide with fear until I see Vincent's face appear in the crack of the doorway.

He pushes the door open, wearing a dark hoodie and a wide smile. "I just got in, and thought I'd heard you in here. I—" he pauses when he sees my face. "Luna?"

I glance back down at the note, my breath hitching as I read the words again. Miss Murder. She's mocking me. Taunting me. And I know, without a shadow of a doubt, that this isn't just about Stephen.

It's about me.

TWENTY-TWO

I've been glued to the news all day, flipping through every local channel, waiting for Stephen's name or face to appear beneath the headline of some unsolved murder. The thought of it makes my stomach twist, but I can't look away. I need confirmation that the manuscript sitting on my desk isn't fiction. It couldn't be. It was about him. My kind, thoughtful, loving Stephen. And until I see it on the screen, the truth will hover in this unbearable limbo, choking me.

But the rational part of me knows I won't see anything. There won't be a body. Janice would have been more thorough this time, knowing the personal connections that could be tied back to us. And with Val Felder's accusations flying across the internet, there's no way she'd risk leaving loose ends. If Stephen's body is out there, no one will find it.

My hair's a mess, tangled from the way I've been gripping it between sobs. Strands cling to my damp cheeks as I sit curled on the couch, clutching a pillow so tightly it feels like it's holding me together. The low murmur of the TV drifts through the room, but it's just noise. My mind is miles away.

Every few minutes, my gaze flicks to my phone on the coffee table. It's silent, the screen dark. I've called Janice more times than I can count, sent text after text, even messaged her Charles Dickens account on Momnt. No replies. No dots showing she's typing. Just silence.

I consider grabbing my keys and driving to her house, but the thought makes my chest tighten. Her message on Momnt was clear. I shouldn't have gone to her house before. And the truth is, I'm too afraid to go again. I'm afraid of what I'd find—or worse, what I wouldn't.

I bury my face in the pillow, the fabric muffling the scream clawing its way out of my throat. She must be laughing at me. Sitting somewhere, savoring this moment, taking pleasure in my desperation. And it's working. For the first time since this nightmare began, Val Felder and the controversy don't even cross my mind. The world outside this house doesn't matter anymore. The only thing I can think about is Stephen.

The person I've already lost.

And the growing fear that Janice isn't finished.

The hum of my mother's machines plays in the background, a steady rhythm that usually comforts me. But now, even that sound feels tainted. Janice has been here—I know it. She left that note, *Retire or Else*. I'm sure of it now, after seeing that latest mocking note.

Except... why would she leave it? If I retire, she loses her purpose. Her income. Unless that doesn't matter to her anymore. Unless she's moved beyond needing me.

A line from the manuscript flashes in my mind, the words sharp and cutting: *He thought he could play detective.*

A thought occurs to me.

What if Stephen wasn't cheating at all? What if after I told him about the controversy, he went to Janice because he suspected she was behind it all? My stomach twists at the thought. What if he was trying to protect me, and I pushed him away?

I shake my head, my fingers curling into the pillow. It's too much. Too many questions. Too many possibilities. I don't know if Stephen was a warning or a consequence. I don't know if this is all some twisted plan of hers to force my hand.

And maybe none of it matters. The only thing I know for certain is that Stephen is dead, and it's my fault. If I'd trusted him—confided in him like any normal girlfriend would—he might still be alive.

"Here, eat this."

Vincent's voice cuts through the haze. I glance up to see him standing behind the couch, a plate of fruit in his hands. My stomach rumbles, and I reluctantly take the plate from him. He sits beside me, offering a sympathetic look as I nibble on a strawberry.

He must have some idea of what's going on. After all, I read that manuscript, then panicked and turned on the news. It wouldn't take a genius to piece together that my books might be connected to real murders. And I'm sure I must have screamed Stephen's name more than once.

But Vincent doesn't look judgmental. He just waits

until I've eaten a few more bites before speaking. "Are you ready to talk?"

I meet his eyes, and a sudden flash of fear courses through me. What if he's next? I'm shocked by how much the thought terrifies me. Somehow, over these last two years, Vincent has become a constant—a comforting presence, even. Because as long as he's here, my mother is okay.

He notices the fear in my eyes and frowns, reaching out to place his hand over mine. His skin is warm, steadying.

"What's wrong, Luna?" he asks.

A dark laugh escapes me. Where do I even start? At the beginning, when I called out to the internet for help and invited a monster into my life? Or here, where I know I'll have to watch helplessly as Stephen's death goes unanswered—and Janice probably pressures me to publish his story. The thought makes my stomach churn.

"Everything," I whisper.

He slides closer, wrapping an arm around me and pulling me into his chest. I let him, burying my face against his shoulder. I hate that I'm betraying Stephen's memory, even now, but I need this. I need him.

"Don't worry," Vincent says softly. "Everything will be okay."

I shake my head, just barely. "You don't know what I'm dealing with."

"I don't need to know. Look at me," he says, pulling back enough to meet my eyes. He gives me a confident smile. "You and your mother are safe with me. Do you believe that?"

Hesitantly, I nod. I'm not sure how he'd protect us from Janice, but I believe him. Somehow, I believe he'll keep us safe.

I wipe my eyes and draw a shaky breath. There's one way to stop all of this, to end it before it gets worse.

"Vincent?"

"Yeah?"

"I think I need to talk to the police."

His body tenses, just slightly, but I notice. My stomach twists again as I look up at him.

"Why?" he asks.

I open my mouth to explain, to tell him everything, but the words catch. I hate myself for it. All these secrets, these lies—they're destroying me. Destroying my life. Destroying the people I care about.

"It's getting to be too much," I manage finally.

He rubs his jaw, grimacing. "I don't know if that's a good idea."

I sit up, my heart sinking. "Why not? What is it?"

He hesitates. "Do you remember how I told you I checked for Stephen's things, and got rid of anything left over like you'd asked?"

I nod slowly, my pulse quickening.

"That wasn't quite the truth. Stephen actually came by while you were out. There were too many things for his Jeep, so he asked me to help him take his stuff to a storage unit."

He pauses.

"There'll be footage of me with him. If you really think something's happened to him, I might be one of the last people to see him alive."

The words hang in the air, sharp and heavy, leaving no space for me to respond. Footage. *One of the last people to see him alive.* My mind spins, torn between disbelief and the suffocating implications of what he's just said.

"Why didn't you tell me this earlier?" I manage, my voice thin and trembling.

Vincent looks down, rubbing the back of his neck. "Because you seem like you have a lot on your plate, and I didn't want to upset you, and..." His eyes meet mine, and there's something in them I can't quite read. "Well, I didn't want to worry you."

"Worry me?" My voice rises, my pulse quickening as I push myself off the couch and pace the room. "Vincent, this isn't something you keep to yourself! Stephen is dead! He's—" The words choke me, the finality of them forcing me to stop. I clutch the back of the couch for support, my breath coming fast and uneven. "He's gone, and I don't even know why. And now you're telling me there's footage of you with him? Do you have any idea how bad this looks?"

"I know," he says softly, still seated, his hands clasped tightly in his lap. "That's why you can't go to the police."

His calm demeanor only fuels my frustration. "Why not? Are you afraid they'll think you had something to do with it?"

"Luna," he says. "Think about what you're saying. You don't trust them any more than I do. They're already looking into you. The second you walk into that station, they'll find a way to cast blame on you. Do you really want to risk that?"

I stop pacing, his words hitting me like a bucket of ice water. He's right. Once the police realized Stephen was missing, they'd throw the whole force at me. It'd be proof enough to give them what they need to dig into everything. They'd blow the controversy open, uncover all the years of lies and half-truths I've built my career on.

My stomach twists and my knees go weak at the thought of what would happen to my mother. I sit back down, my hands trembling in my lap. "I don't know what to do," I whisper.

Vincent sits beside me again, his arm brushing against mine. "You don't have to decide anything right now. Just breathe. One step at a time, okay?"

I nod, even though it feels like I'm suffocating. The walls of the house seem like they're coming down all around me.

"This is all my fault," I murmur. "Everything I've built, everything I've done—it's all a lie. I can't even write my own stories, Vincent. I've been fooling everyone. My fans, my publishers, Stephen—"

"Stop," he says firmly, his tone cutting through my spiraling thoughts. His grip on my hand tightens just enough to hold me in place. "I don't know what you're talking about, but what happened to Stephen isn't your fault. What happened to Val's son isn't your fault."

"You don't understand."

"I don't need to," he says. "What I understand is this —you're smart, and you'll figure this out. You always do."

I want to believe him. I want to take those words and let them soothe the raw edges of my soul. But deep down,

I can't shake the feeling that I don't deserve his faith. Not after everything that's happened.

TWENTY-THREE

The cursor blinks back at me, taunting me once again over the empty document. I remain in my leather chair, staring at it like it's the answer to everything. If I can just figure out how to break through this seemingly impenetrable wall, then the floodgates will open and this'll all be fixed.

Of course, the thought is delusional. Even if I was somehow suddenly able to do the one thing that had plagued me my whole life, it didn't solve my problems. Not a single one of them, actually.

The cops would still be watching me, looking for any sign of truth in the rumor mill that's spun up across social media. Alyssa Lake would still be going forward with her segment, pushing whatever message would resonate with the readers most, no doubt. And Janice, all-important Janice, would still be out there killing and writing her manuscripts, all while complicating my life even further.

Even so, I still want to get just a single line down. I'm sure it'd lift my spirits at the very least, because if I could manage *that*, then I could definitely manage the chaos my life was turning into.

As I sit there, though, the seconds turn to minutes, and the dragging minutes turn to hours—long enough for my body to ache from sitting so long.

I push myself out of the chair with a frustrated sigh, the leather squeaking as I stand. My legs are stiff, my back sore from how long I'd been sitting, and the room feels too small, too confining. Pacing might not solve anything, but at least it's something to do. I can still think of what I want my first line to be. When it comes to me, I can rush back here and type it down before it gets lost. That's what I tell myself, anyways, as I leave the office.

It's not long before I get caught up in the flipping between local news stations and a housewife drama that'll keep my mind distracted. I'm two episodes deep when I hear a knock at the door.

It's soft at first, barely loud enough for me to register. But it comes again, three sharp knocks, firmer this time.

For a moment, I don't move. My body feels rooted to the couch. Could it be Vincent? No, he's still here—somewhere. Janice? My pulse quickens at the thought, but I know that it couldn't be her. She wouldn't knock. Not when she felt comfortable enough to break into my house twice already.

Before I can think through the other options, I hear a loud voice calling through the door.

"Ms. Harrow, it's Detective Hardy. I know you're home. Please come to the door."

I swear under my breath.

Instinctively, I look for some way to escape, but I

catch myself. It's a silly thought. My mother's upstairs and there's no way I can leave her behind. I force myself to get up and take a step, then another, my feet carrying me toward the front door like I'm wading through water.

The knocks come again, harder, like the detective's getting impatient.

I peer through the window, catching a glimpse of the man on my doorstep. He's handsome, in a rugged sort of way. He sighs, exasperated, and looks over his shoulder at his car: a black Lincoln parked next to my Range Rover and Vincent's old Honda. He adjusts the badge clipped to his belt, then sees me looking through the window.

"Ms. Harrow," he says, his tone clipped. "Please open the door."

I grimace, but do as he says.

"Detective," I say, eyes darting past him for a sign of any other cops. "What can I help you with?"

"I called you. Left a voicemail, but you didn't call back."

"Right, yes. I was busy."

His brow lifts a fraction. He clears his throat. "Do you have a moment to talk?"

Every instinct in me screams to say no, to slam the door shut in his face and pretend this isn't happening. But I know better. It *is* happening, and he's not going to go away.

I nod slowly, gripping the edge of the door for support. "What's this about?"

He eyes me for a long minute.

My heart pounds in my chest.

Then he jerks his thumb over his shoulder. "Your Range Rover."

"What about it?"

"Looks pretty banged up."

"Yeah, I uh... I guess so."

He sighs and runs his hand over his face. "Okay, look, let me be a little more straightforward with this. I'm fully aware of who you are, Ms. Harrow, and what kind of stir this could cause in the media given your... fame. But we've received a complaint about a hit and run."

I blink. "What?"

"Yes, a hit and run. Some captured footage revealed the license plate to be yours, and one look at your vehicle tells me everything I need to know."

I want to laugh. "That's what you're here about?"

He frowns. "What else would I be here about?"

"There's a lot of talk going on about me on social media."

He puts a hand up, "Ms. Harrow, if you're referencing concerns brought up by a certain grieving mother, then you don't need to worry. However distasteful it might be to write fiction based on real life events, it isn't illegal. That being said, it would be my advice to avoid too much similarity to police and media reports, out of respect to the grieving families, of course."

Relief floods through me, so sharp and sudden that again, I almost laugh. "I thought you were here to drag me away in cuffs."

The detective chuckles, "Not today, no. But I'll say this. You're lucky. The damage done to the parked car you hit was relatively minor, with most of the damage coming from a pole you scraped against. No injuries."

"That's good, then!"

"It is. But in the future, you should refrain from speeding, Ms. Harrow. I would hate to be the bearer of bad news to your family if something unfortunate happened."

My lips spread into a smile. "I'm not a very good driver, I'm sorry. I'll make sure to be more careful. So... what happens next?"

Hardy pulls a small pad from his jacket, scribbles something down, and hands me the torn sheet. "This is your citation. Just pay the fine within thirty days, and that's it. No court, no additional penalties. You'll receive a letter soon about damages owed to the owner of the car you struck—they'd like to keep this quiet as well—but otherwise, that's it. Nice and straightforward."

I take the paper, staring down at the bold, printed letters and the fine amount. It's laughable compared to the mountain of problems I've been imagining. For the first time in what feels like weeks, my shoulders loosen. "That's... really it?"

"That's it," he confirms, his tone softening. "Like I said, I'm keeping this quiet. No press, no spectacle. My wife wouldn't forgive me if I turned this into something bigger than it needs to be."

The mention of his wife brings a faint, awkward smile to my lips. "She's a fan?"

"A big one," he says with a nod. "She calls your books her guilty pleasure. Personally, I'm more of a sports guy, but hey, everyone has their thing."

For a moment, I almost feel normal. Like this is just a casual exchange with a stranger, not a conversation with a detective at my door.

"Well, tell her thank you," I say, clutching the citation tightly. "I appreciate the discretion."

Hardy chuckles lightly, stepping back toward the porch. "Will do. And Ms. Harrow?"

"Yes?"

His expression shifts slightly, more serious now, though not unkind. "If there's anything else weighing on you—anything you're not saying—you should know that it's better to handle it quietly, like this, than to let it spiral into something worse."

The relief in my chest falters for a second, but I force myself to nod. "I understand. And there's nothing else."

He studies me for a long moment, then nods. "Alright. Take care of yourself, Ms. Harrow. And good luck with your writing."

I watch him walk back to his car, his footsteps steady against the gravel. The red glow of his taillights fades as he drives away, leaving me standing in the doorway, the crisp paper still clutched in my hand.

The door shuts, and a sound bursts out of me—half-laugh, half-sob, as though my body can't decide which emotion to latch onto first. It's ridiculous, really, how light I feel. For days, I've been convinced there was a prison cell waiting for me on the back of Val's accusations. But now, for the first time, it feels like I can breathe.

No legal trouble. Not yet, anyway. At least, not until there's actual proof of what Janice has done.

Stick to the routine. Don't question the process.

I hate to admit it, but she was right. For now, the routine is what's been keeping me safe.

Not that I'm in the clear, yet. The future of Miss Murder is still dangling by a thread, and Alyssa Lake's upcoming segment feels like a blade poised to cut it. Legal trouble or not, if the fans turn against me after her broadcast, then what? I shudder to think about it—what it would mean for me, for my mother. For everything.

But I don't let my mind spiral down that path. Not tonight. Not now. I'll take this win, and celebrate it with the one person who's been here through all of it.

"Vincent!" I call, my voice echoing through the house as I make my way down the hall. There's no answer.

I stop by my mother's room, pressing a soft kiss to her forehead. Her eyes are still locked onto the ceiling, that strange look still lingering there, one I can't quite name. Fear? Worry? I squeeze her hand gently, whispering, "Everything's going to be alright." Whether I'm trying to comfort her or convince myself, I don't know.

But I mean it. Tonight, I'm letting myself believe it.

I step out of her room, closing the door quietly behind me, and continue my search. "Vincent!" I call again, louder this time.

The house is quiet. My footsteps feel loud against the hardwood as I check the kitchen, the living room, the guest bedroom where he's moved in. Nothing. Not a trace of him. But I know he's here. His car is parked in the driveway.

I look out back and I see that the light to the suite out back is on. He must be out there. I head outside with the smile still on my face and rap my knuckles against his door.

The gentle breeze blows through my hair as I wait for him to answer. I close my eyes, leaning into the breeze. God, it feels so good. I swear that if I get through all of this, then I'll never take another thing for granted ever again.

"Vincent!" I call again, this time in a sing-song voice. "Hurry up, open the door."

He doesn't. I let out a heavy sigh. Where is he? It's not really like him, to suddenly be missing.

I freeze.

Was it possible that Janice had decided to come around again, somehow catching him unaware while I was distracted? I know that he promised me that everything was going to be okay, but he didn't know what she was capable of. I hadn't ever really told him. I swear under my breath and jiggle the doorknob, but it doesn't open. It's only then that I reach for the keys in my pocket.

When he was first brought on, he'd asked if he would have complete privacy to the suite. It was normal, wanting to know if your employer was going to bust into your personal space or not. I'd told him I never would, and that he had the only key to the suite. It was a lie, of course. I'd snuck into his suite occasionally in the early days, mostly to make sure that there was no hidden drugs or pileup of empty beer cans. Had to make sure that my mother was safe with whoever was taking care of her, after all.

So it was with only a little bit of shame that when I opened the door, I looked on with some familiarity. The place is immaculate, as it always is. The kitchen counters are spotless, the couch pillows perfectly fluffed. But there's a strange stillness in the air. I glance toward his bedroom door, which is slightly ajar, the faint glow of a bedside lamp spilling into the hallway.

That was the light I'd seen from inside the house.

"Vincent?" I call out again, though I know there won't be an answer.

Pushing the door open fully, I step inside. The bed is made, not a wrinkle in sight, and the faint scent of his cologne lingers in the air. I scan the room and its attached bathroom, but he isn't there.

Maybe he went running?

But that possibility is quickly killed when I see his running shoes sitting neatly by the door. I stand in his living room, biting my lip with worry.

It's hard to describe the unease sitting in the pit of my stomach, but I'm starting to think that something bad has happened to him. What if that look in my mother's eyes *was* fear? What if that was her attempt to tell me that something had happened to him?

With shaking hands, I reach for my phone and open up my past text messages with Janice. I type out a quick message.

Did you do something to Vincent? My mother's caretaker?

My finger hovers over the send button, conscious of how exactly this could go wrong. If she *hadn't* done something to him, then I was putting him in the spotlight, painting him as someone I cared about. But I can't get rid of this nagging feeling that something *has* happened to him.

Holding my breath, I press send the text.

A half-second later, I hear the subtle sound of a muted notification. I frown and head toward the bedroom, where I thought the sound came from. I look around, but don't see what made the sound.

I glance down at my phone again, my heart starting to sputter in my chest. I send another text message.

Janice?

The notification sounds again, coming from his bedside table. The air is tight, so tight that it feels impossible to breathe as I go to the table and slide open the drawer.

Neatly spaced inside is the same phone I'd seen Janice use when we met up in the café. And right beside it is another phone. But this one is more familiar.

It's Stephen's.

TWENTY-FOUR

My hands move instinctively, shoving the phones back into the drawer with trembling fingers. I slam it shut, the sound far louder than I intended, and wince at the noise. My pulse hammers in my ears, my breaths coming short and fast. I wipe my palms against my thighs, trying to steady myself, but the air feels too thick, too heavy to breathe properly.

It didn't take two guesses to know why Janice's and Stephen's phones were here. But now isn't the time to question it. Not here, not while I'm still in his suite.

I glance around quickly, making sure everything looks the same as when I arrived. The pillows on the couch are untouched, the kitchen counter spotless, and the faint glow of the bedside lamp casts the same golden hue. Nothing out of place—except me.

With one last sweep of the room, I grab the doorknob and close the door behind me. The breeze brushes against my skin, but it does nothing to calm the heat crawling up the back of my neck. I lock the door behind me, slipping the key back into my pocket, and make my way to the house as casually as I can manage.

A light turns on in the kitchen, and I force my pace to stay measured as I reach the back door and push it open.

"Luna?" Vincent's voice startles me, and I whip around to see him standing in the hallway, a faint sheen of sweat glistening on his forehead. His sleeves are rolled up, his dark hair tousled as if he's been running his hands through it. He tilts his head slightly, a curious smile tugging at his lips. "What were you doing out back?"

I freeze for half a second, but my mind scrambles for an answer. "Oh," I say, forcing a casual laugh. "I went to knock on your door. I wanted to see where you were."

He pauses, studying me with eyes that seem to pierce straight through me. "Why would I be out there?"

"What?"

"Did you forget? I'm in the guest bedroom now."

I swallow nervously, before forcing a laugh and waving a hand dismissively, "I didn't forget. I just saw the light on out there, thought you might be getting something."

He frowns. "Didn't realize I left the light on."

I shrug, trying to match his easy demeanour.

"Well, here I am. Hope I didn't worry you. I just needed some fresh air. Clear my head, you know?"

"Yeah," I say, my voice barely above a whisper. My hands grip the edge of the counter as I steady myself. "Of course."

He takes a long drink, then leans against the counter,

studying me. "What about you? You look like you've seen a ghost."

I force another laugh. I needed to change the topic. Fast. "Actually, I've got some good news."

His expression brightens. "Oh?"

"That detective who left the voicemail? He came by earlier. Apparently all of that scare was about the Range Rover. Nothing serious, just a ticket for a hit-and-run."

The words feel hollow as they leave my mouth, the relief I'd felt earlier now tangled with raw fear. But Vincent doesn't seem to notice. His face breaks into a wide grin, his shoulders relaxing as he sets the water bottle on the counter.

"That's amazing," he says, his excitement genuine. "You must feel incredible."

I nod, forcing a smile to match his. "Yeah. It's... a relief."

He steps closer, resting a hand on my shoulder. "We should celebrate. You deserve it."

The suggestion catches me off guard, but I nod quickly, desperate to keep the facade intact. "You're right. We should."

His smile widens, and he moves toward the liquor cabinet. "How about a drink? Something strong. You could use it."

I bite the inside of my cheek, my stomach twisting as I watch him pour two glasses, my mind racing to piece everything together. Janice being the serial killer made sense– too much sense. But Vincent? That didn't fit. I couldn't connect the dots, not completely. And yet, he had both Janice's and Stephen's phones.

Maybe Vincent had lied about Stephen coming by the house, or maybe it was true and that's how he caught him. Either way, Stephen was dead. That much I knew. And Janice? She'd never shown up when we were supposed to meet. I hadn't seen her in person for weeks—only her texts. Texts that, now that I thought about it, could have come from him.

Was she dead too?

"To moving past all this," Vincent says, raising his glass with a grin.

I clink mine against his, the sound too loud in the quiet kitchen. "To moving past this."

Drinks with Vincent stretched late into the night, but there was no escaping it. I had to keep up the image—the image of someone utterly unsuspecting, someone who couldn't possibly fathom that he might be a serial killer. At first, it was hard, my hands trembling slightly as I raised the glass to my lips, but the alcohol eventually worked its magic, calming my nerves just enough to make it easier. Pretending came naturally to me. After all, I was Miss Murder, and nobody suspected me of the truth so far. Well, not until Val Felder knocked on my doorstep.

When Vincent finally polishes off his last drink and calls it a night, he disappears into his room, leaving me to retreat to mine. But even as I sit here, the edges of my mind still slightly frayed from the alcohol, I'm more sober than I've ever been. Sober because I know the truth. And knowing the truth has a way of sharpening everything around you, even when you've been drinking.

I wait an hour. A long, excruciating hour, the ticking of the clock on my wall a steady reminder of how little time I might have. My pacing feels endless, back and forth across the bedroom floor until I'm sure I've worn a path into the rug. At last, I can't take it anymore.

Carefully, I slip out the door, the hinges groaning far louder than I'd like in the silence of the house. The sound makes me freeze, my breath catching in my throat as I wait, listening for any signs that Vincent might have stirred. But nothing comes.

I tiptoe down the hallway, my bare feet barely making a sound against the cool floor. My heart thuds painfully in my chest as I reach his door and press my ear against it. For a moment, there's nothing, just the muffled sounds of my mother's equipment down the hall. But then I hear it—the soft, steady rhythm of his snores. He's asleep. Deeply asleep, judging by the sound of it. And after all the drinks he had tonight, I'm confident he won't be waking up anytime soon.

Of course he feels at ease. Why wouldn't he? The police aren't on his trail. As far as Vincent knows, everything is under control, the world oblivious once again.

But I'm not oblivious. Not anymore.

I grab my keys off the kitchen counter, slipping them into my pocket as quietly as possible. My shoes are waiting by the door, and I ease them on, careful not to let the soles squeak against the tile. I have to be careful not to wake Vincent, because if I do, I'm not sure I'll have a good explanation for why I'm sneaking out in the middle of the night.

But I had to do this. There was something I needed to know.

The cool night air brushes against my skin as I step outside. The Range Rover looms in the driveway, its bulk casting long shadows in the faint moonlight. I grip the door handle and ease it open, the faint squeal of the hinge making me wince. Sliding into the driver's seat, I shift the car into neutral, holding my breath as I release the brake.

The tires crunch against the gravel, louder than I'd expected, and my pulse spikes. I glance toward the house, waiting for a light to turn on. When it doesn't come, I breathe a sigh of relief.

Slowly, with my hands braced against the edge of the doorframe, I begin to push, straining to get the car moving. It's heavier than I thought it'd be, my muscles burning with the effort. But I can't start the engine here—not with Vincent sleeping just inside.

The car creeps forward, the gravel protesting beneath its weight, and I'm left panting for air as I fight to keep it moving. My arms ache, my breath coming in shallow gasps, but finally—finally—I get it onto the road.

I climb back inside, slam the door shut, and turn the key in the ignition. The engine hums to life, and I glance over my shoulder toward the house. The windows are dark, no lights flickering on to signal I've been caught.

I'm safe. For now.

The Range Rover rolls down the quiet streets, the hum of the tires against the pavement the only sound. It doesn't take long to reach Janice's house. The sight of it sends a shiver down my spine. It's still perfect, just like before—too perfect. The neatly trimmed hedges, the pristine white shutters, the flower beds arranged in flawless symmetry. But tonight, the house carries a different energy. There's an edge to it now.

I park across the street, the engine idling as I stare at the house. My breath fogs the glass as I exhale, my fingers tightening on the steering wheel. The last time I was here, there was someone there with me. It must have been Vincent. There's no denying it anymore.

I swallow hard, my eyes fixed on the darkened windows. What had happened to Janice? When I was here last, she must have still been alive. She had to be. Why else would I have gotten a text saying that we needed to meet. Maybe Vincent had been looking for her, and that's why he was in the house when I broke in.

Of course, she could be long dead with her body already rotting. I had to acknowledge the possibility that maybe Vincent just messaged me from her phone so that I wouldn't think anything strange had happened.

I'm not sure I buy that idea though. My gut tells me she was living when she texted me. *Was.*

I get out of the vehicle and quietly shut the door behind me. The last thing I needed was for the nosey neighbor to look outside and see me again.

When I cross the road and reach the front door, it's locked. I try to turn the knob, shoulder it open, but the door doesn't budge. Even when I cut around to the back of the house to try the back door, it's locked. But I wasn't about to be turned away now. I needed to know the truth.

Desperation claws at me as I scan the yard for

something—anything—that might give me a way inside. My gaze falls on a small pile of rocks nestled beneath one of the garden bushes, their jagged edges glinting faintly in the moonlight. I crouch down, sifting through them with trembling fingers until I find the biggest one. It's rough and solid, and it feels heavy enough to do the job.

Clutching the rock, I creep back to the window, my breath catching in my throat as I raise it above my head. For a second, I hesitate. Then, with a swift motion, I bring it down hard against the corner of the glass.

The shattering sound splits the night, but not as loud as I feared. My heart pounds as I freeze, waiting for the inevitable—the neighbor's back door creaking open, her suspicious face peering over the fence. But the seconds tick by, and the yard remains quiet. No movement, no lights flicking on.

I breathe a shallow sigh of relief, knocking aside the larger shards of glass still clinging to the window frame. Careful to not cut myself, I reach through the jagged opening, my fingers fumbling with the lock. The door swings open a moment later, its hinges groaning softly in the night.

The house feels colder than I remember. Darker. The pristine neatness that once felt staged now feels more oppressive. For once, I'm grateful for my aphantasia. I can't picture Vincent stalking these halls, can't see him dragging a screaming Janice by her ankle, her nails clawing at the hardwood floor. Instead, I'm met with only the blissful, saving darkness.

Still, my skin prickles, a chill crawling up my arms as

I step inside. My shoes crunch faintly on the glass scattered behind me.

"Hello?" I call out, my voice low and harsh, a whisper swallowed by the heavy air.

Nothing.

The quiet is thick, pressing against my ears, but this time, unlike before, I find comfort in it. There's no dread that Vincent will respond in place of her, and no irrational hope that her voice will call back from somewhere deeper in the house. I know what I'll find here. Or more accurately, what I won't.

Janice isn't here. She hasn't been for a while.

I push further into the house, doing my best to ignore the framed photos hanging on the walls. It's weird. I can almost feel Janices's eyes following me from them, urging me along toward... *something*.

When I reach the basement door, I push it open and am greeted with that familiar scent of ink. With a flip of a switch, light floods the stairs.

The stairs creak as I make my way down to the basement, the smell of ink growing stronger with each step. My stomach twists. This is where it was last time. The typewriter. If I find it, maybe I'll finally get some answers.

At first glance, the basement looks just like the last time I left it. But looking closer, I see that's not quite true. The books are sitting askew, almost like someone's gone through them in a rush searching for something. Something about that feels wrong.

My eyes go straight to the desk. My breath catches as I crouch down, reaching underneath. My heart pounds as I fumble along the smooth wood, searching for the hidden latch. Where is it? My fingers finally brush against the familiar groove, and I pull it open. The panel clicks, sliding aside, and I reach inside. But my hand hits nothing but empty space.

No. That can't be right.

I crouch lower, stretching my arm further. My fingers graze something hard and cold, shoved way to the back. The typewriter. Why is it so far in? My muscles strain as I drag it out and set it on the desk, my breath coming fast.

The case looks the same. But something feels... off. It takes me a minute to realize why. The dark, rusty streaks of blood are gone now. It's been cleaned.

I flip it open, my hands trembling.

Nothing.

The clippings, the crime articles—they're gone, too. I sift through the mesh pocket, but it's empty. My chest tightens as I step back, staring at the typewriter like it might explain itself. It doesn't.

This doesn't feel right.

I turn away from it, my eyes surveying the books around me. Vincent's been down here. I'm sure of it. He must have cleaned out this space to make sure that if the cops ever came here, there would be no ties back to him.

My gaze lands on a book resting on the bookshelf.

Don't Breathe Twice.

I frown. That hadn't been there the last time I'd come. It takes a stool for me to reach it, but my fingers close over the spine and pull it off the shelf.

A folded sheet of paper flutters out, seesawing through the air until it hit the ground. I rush to pick it up.

The letter is slightly crumpled and the ink is smeared, as if it had been typed and folded in a hurry.

But even so, I can see that it's addressed to me.

Luna,

If you're reading this, then I'm already dead. I'm guessing you know that.

I don't have much time, so I'll keep this short. You need to know the truth—all of it.

When you told Stephen about the poor, grieving mother that came out with her suspicions, he came to me, thinking that maybe if I helped him, we could piece together the threads nobody's noticed and figure out a way to protect you. But he didn't know that I wasn't just editing your books. I wrote them. Every single one of them.

I didn't want to. God, I didn't want to. But Vincent gave me no choice. He's a monster, Luna, and he's been in control from the very beginning. He blackmailed me, threatened to kill my parents. That's why I reached out to you to work with you. Because he was always there, watching, making sure I did exactly what he wanted.

I wrote everything he told me to. Sitting at crime scenes, typewriter in my lap, breathing in the stench of blood. He forced me to document his murders, turning his horrors into those twisted thrillers everyone loves. The murder scenes in your books? They're not fiction. They're real. Every single one of them.

And he pinned them on you.

When Stephen came to me, I thought maybe it was my chance to stop Vincent. I thought maybe the public atten-

tion would scare him off, make him think twice about continuing this nightmare. That's why I left the Retire or Else *letter for him. I thought I could threaten him, that he would back down and all of this could finally end.*

But it was a horrible mistake. He didn't stop. He never does.

Stephen must have figured it out. That's why he's dead. Vincent doesn't leave loose ends, Luna. And now? You're his biggest loose end.

Please, don't make the same mistake I did. Don't let him control you. Don't let him turn you into his puppet the way he did with me. You have a chance to stop him. Go to the police. Take this letter, the typewriter—anything you can find—and use it as evidence.

I know you think you're trapped. I thought the same thing. But there's still a way out. You just have to be brave enough to take it.

And Luna, whatever you do, don't underestimate him. He's more dangerous than you think.

— Janice

The letter slips from my hands and flutters to the floor, but I barely notice. My knees feel weak, and I grab the edge of the desk to steady myself as her words crash over me.

Janice wasn't just Miss Murder. It was her *and* Vincent. He delivered dark inspiration, and she wrote the words. He was the one who masterminded this, who took my plea for help and twisted it into something monstrous.

I dig my fingers into my scalp, strands of my hair

twisting around them as I squeeze. Who was I here, but the name, the face, the *scapegoat?*

The room feels colder, the shadows in the corners stretching further, darker. My breath comes in shallow bursts, and I feel like I'm standing on the edge of a cliff, the ground crumbling beneath me.

I did it for you.

Janice believes that Vincent doesn't leave loose ends. But what if I wasn't a loose end? Maybe Vincent really thinks he's helping me, by taking care of my mother and giving me the life I'd only ever dreamed of having by using Janice's words.

The thought is nauseating. I swallow hard, my gaze dropping to the typewriter sitting on the desk, its keys gleaming under the dim light. This is the only thing that might save me.

My hands shake as I slam the typewriter case shut, the latch clicking into place with a sharp snap. I tuck the letter into my jacket pocket, my fingers brushing against the crumpled paper in an attempt to reassure myself that it's still there. Then, with one last glance around the room, I grab the typewriter and head for the stairs.

Every step protests under my weight as I climb back to the main floor, my pulse thundering in my ears. I needed to be back home before Vincent woke up and realized I wasn't there. That was dead clear.

The cool night air hits my face as I step outside, and I draw a deep breath, trying to calm my pounding heart. The Range Rover is parked exactly where I left it. I hurry across the yard, the typewriter digging into my side as I clutch it tight against me.

I open the door, slide into the driver's seat, and place the typewriter carefully on the passenger seat. My hands are still as I start the engine. Janice was worried about me underestimating him. But she and Vincent both made a mistake. They underestimated *me*.

I glance back at the house one last time, the dark windows staring back at me like empty eyes.

And then I drive.

TWENTY-FIVE

The next morning, I sit at the kitchen table, dressed in a simple hoodie and sweatpants. My hands wrap around a warm coffee cup, and the heat seeps into my palms. It does little to thaw the cold dread settling in my chest. My eyes sting, and I'm sure they're bloodshot, though a few drops of Visine have masked the evidence. Vincent doesn't need to know that I barely slept. He's sharp—sharper than I ever realized—and the last thing I want is for him to get any ideas.

It's strange, sitting here knowing that at any moment, a serial killer will emerge from my guest bedroom. A man who had somehow woven himself into the fabric of my life so seamlessly that I hadn't noticed until it was too late. He blackmailed Janice into turning his murders into bestselling thrillers and positioned her to be my editor, set himself up as my mother's caretaker, and now, he was standing in the shadows of my career, making sure everything stayed on track.

I take a sip of coffee, the bitterness grounding me for

a moment. My thoughts drift to Janice, and I can't help but wonder what he held over her that kept her trapped for so long. But it doesn't matter now. She's gone.

What's even stranger, though, is that I'm still letting him take care of my mother. Every rational part of me screams that it's insane, that I should have figured out a way to get rid of him overnight. But deep down, I know the truth. There really isn't much I can do. Finding another caretaker at a moment's notice would be impossible. Worse, it would tip him off.

And if there's one thing I'm sure of, it's that Vincent wouldn't hesitate to kill to protect himself. If he sensed that I was onto him, if he even suspected that I'd broken from the routine he's so carefully constructed, I'd end up being his next story. I have a feeling about that.

But as much as it terrifies me, I also can't deny that he's good at what he does. Better than anyone else I've met, including the doctors at the hospital. My mother is doing well under his care, and whether I like it or not, I have to let it continue until I deal with things.

Besides, he's never hurt her. Not once. If anything, he's proven that he cares about her almost as much as I do. As twisted as it sounds, I don't think he'd hurt her anytime soon.

The screen on my phone lights up, pulling my attention away from the hallway where I'm half-expecting Vincent to appear. It's a notification from Alyssa Lake's profile, announcing the date for the segment I'm supposed to appear in—*The Truth About Miss Murder*. My stomach twists as I realize it's just ten days away. Ten days sounds like a lot, but I know how fast time slips by, especially when you're distracted by the small problem of having a serial killer living under your roof.

I shake my head. No. I can't think about Alyssa right now. I need to focus on what's right in front of me.

As if on cue, I hear the soft groan of his door, followed by the faint pad of footsteps on the wooden floor. My breath catches as his tired face appears, his dark hair tousled, his eyes bloodshot. He gives me a smile that's warm and easy—too easy.

"Good morning," he says, his voice gravelly from sleep. "You're up already. Didn't expect that."

The statement makes my shoulders stiffen, my mind instantly overanalyzing. Why wouldn't he expect me to be up early? But then it clicks—last night. The drinks. He thinks I was just as drunk as he was. I relax, my smile coming more easily now.

"Busy day ahead," I say, keeping my tone light, my face calm. Pretend. It's what I've been doing for a long time now.

"Oh, yeah?" he asks, turning to the fridge and pulling out the orange juice. He pours himself a glass, running a hand through his messy hair like everything about this moment is completely normal. "What do you have planned?"

"Errands, mostly," I answer, keeping my voice casual. "I need to get groceries."

He turns to face me, leaning back against the counter, his gaze locking onto mine. Something about the way he's looking at me sends a ripple of unease through my stomach, like he's trying to see straight through me.

"I can take care of that," he says smoothly. "You've got a lot on your plate."

"No, it's alright," I say quickly, forcing a wider smile. "I want to handle it."

"What about your work?" he asks, his tone light but probing.

I blink. "My work?"

He shrugs, taking a sip of orange juice. "Didn't you have another manuscript you wanted to publish?"

The hairs on the back of my neck rise, my fingers tightening around the edge of the counter. Another manuscript? Did he already find someone else to fill Janice's role? Was there another typewritten story waiting on my desk right now that I hadn't seen?

My voice is sharper than I intend as I answer, "I'm not sure what you're talking about."

"You said something about it last night," he says casually. "A short story?"

Relief trickles in, but it doesn't ease the gnawing unease in my gut. He's talking about Stephen's story. I force a laugh, though it comes out stiff. "Did I?"

I really don't think I did.

He nods, his expression unreadable. "You said it might be some of your best work yet."

There's a pressure against my chest, and it's suddenly harder to breathe. Is he taunting me? Does he know? Or is it possible that I drank more than I realized and actually said that? If I did, what else had I said?

He crosses the kitchen and sits down at the table. But he doesn't take his usual spot across from me. Instead, he sits right next to me. Close. Too close. I can feel the warmth radiating off him, his knee almost brushing against mine. My breath hitches as I glance at him, waiting for him to say something, to do something. But he doesn't. He just smiles softly, that easy, unbothered smile of his, and sips his orange juice like nothing's out of the ordinary.

My gaze drops to his hands, and a shiver runs through me. I try to picture them drenched in blood, fingers tight around the handle of a knife as he drives it into someone's chest—again and again. But all I get is that familiar black void. Instead, I'm left staring at those same hands, so calm and clean, as if they couldn't possibly belong to a killer.

But the evidence is there. The phones in his suite. The letter from Janice. Everything I've uncovered points to Vincent. And yet, none of it makes seeing him as a ruthless murderer any easier.

I wonder how many lives he's taken. How high his body count is. It has to be at least as many as the books I've published—each featuring a single, brutal murder. But I doubt it started there. If *The Janitor* was really his first kill, it would have been sloppy. Hesitant. A mess of nerves and mistakes. But it wasn't. It was executed with a level of control that only comes with experience. It was like killing had already become second nature to him.

Even if he *had* started then, though, that would already make him one of the most prolific serial killers in history. Right up there with the BTK Killer, Ted Bundy, and John Wayne Gacy.

And yet, here he is. Sitting next to me, calm as anything, drinking orange juice.

I down the rest of my coffee and push my chair back, the legs scraping loudly against the hardwood floor. The sound cuts through the silence, drawing his attention.

"I need to get going," I say, forcing a casual tone. "Get the groceries out of the way."

Vincent glances at the clock, his expression thoughtful. "Dillon's doesn't open until eight."

Damn it. I'm getting sloppy.

"Oh, I know," I say, shrugging that I hope looks natural. "I just thought I'd drive around a bit. See if it jogs any ideas about... book stuff."

He takes another sip from his glass, but his eyes don't leave mine. There's a flicker of something there—something dark and unreadable—before he speaks. "Is it something I can help with?"

"No," I blurt out, way too fast.

His brow arches, a silent question hanging in the air between us.

I clear my throat, forcing a tight smile. "This is for me to handle. Just me."

Vincent doesn't say anything else, but his gaze lingers on me a moment too long. My pulse races as I pick up my coffee mug and carry it to the sink, rinsing it with shaky hands. I can feel his eyes on my back, like he's trying to read the thoughts spinning in my head.

"You sure you don't need me to pick up the groceries?" he asks.

"I'm sure," I say without turning around. "I've got it covered."

I dry my hands, grab my keys, and force a smile as I glance back at him. He's still seated at the table, leaning back in his chair, watching me like he's waiting for me to crack under the pressure.

"Well, I'd better get going," I say, trying to keep my tone light.

He nods, lifting his glass of orange juice in a small, almost mocking salute. "Drive safe."

I don't let myself hesitate. I grab my bag and head for the door, shutting it behind me with a deliberate click. Only when I'm standing on the front porch, with the morning sun warming my face, do I let out the breath I'd been holding.

I slide into the Range Rover and start the engine, but I don't pull out right away. My hands grip the steering wheel tightly as I stare at the house. The truth is, I don't have any intention of going to Dillon's or running errands. That was never the plan.

Because there's someone I need to see first. Someone I've been avoiding since this all started. Someone who might be just who I need to fix everything.

It's long past time to come face-to-face with the woman who set this all in motion.

Val Felder.

TWENTY-SIX

It wasn't exactly hard to find out where Val Felder lived. A quick Google search led me to an old article where she'd posted her contact details—mailing address included—hoping someone, anyone, with information about her son's death would reach out. I'm guessing nobody ever did. Maybe nobody even read the article. Things like that had a way of getting swallowed whole by the internet, drowned in a sea of louder, more urgent stories. A million screaming voices, all clamoring for attention, until yours became just another whisper.

And judging by the state of Val's house, that's exactly what happened.

The garden is dead, the flowers long withered and choked by weeds. The grass spills over onto the cracked walkway leading to her front door. The roof sags on one side, the shingles warped from years of neglect. I can almost picture the rain seeping through, soaking the insulation, inviting mold to creep its way inside. Does she notice it? Does she care? Probably not. Grief has a way of dulling the edges of everything else, leaving only the sharp sting of what you've lost.

I sigh, leaning back in my seat. If only those million screaming voices had drowned out my Momnt message from more than two years ago, then maybe none of this would have happened. Vincent—my mysterious Charles Dickens—never would have found me. He never would have killed Stephen. Never would have blackmailed Janice, turned her into his unwilling accomplice, then killed her too.

I shake my head and slide lower, letting the seat cradle me like it could somehow hide me. My hood is flipped up, pulled low over my face, as if that could disguise me or my Range Rover, which sticks out on this street like a sore thumb. Even with the damage along the side of the vehicle, it's far too polished, too out of place on a road like this. But I can't do much about that.

I've been waiting for a while now, watching for Val like a stalker. If there was any chance of fixing things, I had to work *with* Val, not against her. Especially now that I knew what Vincent really was. But she hasn't come out yet.

My fingers drum against the steering wheel, my eyes glued to the cracked front door of Val's house. The minutes stretch, each one more unbearable than the last. I consider getting out, knocking on the door, but the thought of facing her without a plan makes my chest tighten. No, I'll wait. She'll come out eventually. She has to.

I glance down at my phone, checking the time.

A sharp knock against my window jolts me so hard

that my seatbelt digs into my chest. My head snaps up, and there she is—Val Felder, inches from the glass. My heart slams against my ribs as I take her in: pale, sunken features, dark hollows beneath her eyes, and a gun glinting faintly in her hand.

I lower the window slowly, the cold air slicing through the cabin of the car as my breath catches in my throat.

"Why are you here?" Her voice is raw, cracked. But her eyes—they're black and hollow, filled with a tortured intensity that makes it impossible to look away.

I swallow hard, trying to steady my voice. "I came to talk."

Her lip curls, the gun lifting slightly, her grip tightening. "Now you want to talk? After weeks of silence? You're a professional liar, Luna Harrow. The whole world knows that now. And so do I." She raises the gun another fraction, the threat clear. "You should leave before it's too late."

My stomach twists, but I force myself to hold her gaze. "Val, I wasn't ignoring you. I just... I needed time."

"Time?" The word drips with venom. "Time for what? To figure out how to spin this? To keep lying to everyone?"

"No." The word comes out sharper than I mean it to, and I quickly soften my tone. "I needed time because I've been trying to find the truth."

Her lips press into a thin, unforgiving line. For a moment, she says nothing, her eyes locked onto mine. Then, her voice drops. "The truth?"

I nod, my heart pounding in my chest. "What if I told you I found out who did it?"

Her expression doesn't change at first. But then, as the seconds stretch, grief and anger twist her face into something almost unrecognizable. "You're a cruel woman, Luna Harrow. I should put a bullet in your head right now." Her voice trembles, her pain raw. "But I won't. Because I want to see your face when you lose everything. That's the only thing keeping me alive."

She taps the muzzle of the gun against the window frame, the hollow sound reverberating like a death knell. My spine tingles, a cold sweat breaking out on my skin.

"You've got one minute to get off my road," she says, her voice firm and steady now. "Or I'll call the police."

"Okay," I say, keeping my tone calm even as my pulse races. "But if I leave, you'll never know who did it. Who killed your son."

Her jaw tightens, and she shakes her head, turning away.

"Wait!" I call out, desperation creeping into my voice.

She keeps walking.

"They're all murders," I blurt.

That stops her. Her shoulders stiffen, and a heartbeat later, she turns back, her face unreadable.

"What did you just say?" she asks, her voice low and dangerous.

"Every single one of my books," I say, my voice shaking as I realize there's no way to take this back now. "They're not based on murders. They are murders. Real ones."

Her expression hardens, her eyes narrowing as if she's waiting for me to laugh, to take it back. But when I don't, the suspicion flickers into something darker. "What are you saying?"

"I'm saying there's a real killer behind my books. And just like your son, he's targeted someone for every single one of them."

Her breath hitches, a sharp, shuddering sound, and I can see the moment it clicks for her. "*Don't Breathe Twice* wasn't written off the police report," she says, her voice barely audible.

I shake my head. "No, it wasn't."

Her gun lifts again, this time aimed squarely at me. "Then that means you knew. That means you've been complicit this whole time. That makes you a murderer too."

"No!" The word bursts out of me, my hands flying up in surrender. "I didn't know, Val. I didn't write my books."

The gun wavers slightly. "What?"

"I have aphantasia," I say, the confession tumbling out. "I can't even picture things. Someone else wrote the books. I just published them."

She looks at me with confusion. Down the road, headlights appear, a car slowly turning onto the street. Val glances toward it, her grip tightening on the gun, before she looks back at me. I can see the conflict in her eyes now, the struggle between wanting to pull the trigger and needing to know more.

"You know who killed my son?" she asks, her voice soft but razor-sharp.

I nod, my breath shaky.

She lowers the gun slightly, her hands trembling now. "Then you'd better come in."

I get out of my Range Rover and follow her inside, preparing myself to be presented with what could only be described as a hoarder's dream. But to my surprise, it is nothing at all like I expect.

The inside of the house is simple, almost minimalist, but there's a strange coziness to it. The furniture is mismatched—an old armchair with faded floral upholstery, a worn leather recliner, a coffee table that looks like it's been sanded and stained a dozen times over. Everything is functional, but it carries a quiet charm, like each piece has been here long enough to become part of the house itself.

The faint smell of lavender and something citrusy lingers in the air, masking any hint of damp. But as my eyes adjust, I catch sight of a dark patch near the corner of the ceiling, where mold's settled in. Despite that fact, the house feels... lived-in. Loved, even.

My gaze catches on the walls, where photos hang in neat, intentional rows. Most are of the same young man, his dark hair swept to the side, a grin that lights up his whole face. He's holding trophies in some of them, in others he's standing with Val, her arm wrapped tightly around his shoulders. Cody Felder. It has to be him.

Judging by the light in her eyes in the photos, he was her everything. And Vincent took him, reducing him to a character in a book that readers devoured without a second thought.

No wonder she wanted justice for him so badly.

"Take a seat," Val says, her voice cutting through my thoughts. She gestures toward a pair of chairs positioned by the fireplace. The fire has burned low, little more than glowing embers now, but the heat radiates outward, filling the room.

I nod, sinking into the armchair. It's surprisingly comfortable, the kind of comfort that only comes with age. The fabric is soft, worn thin in places, but it hugs me as I settle back. Across from me, Val disappears into the kitchen, taking her gun with her.

She returns a moment later, balancing a tray with two mugs of tea and a small plate of biscuits. She places it on the coffee table between us, then hands me a mug.

I raise a brow, surprised by the display of hospitality. Not to mention that this all seemed like something out of a British film.

"Thanks," I say, reaching for one of the biscuits. "I've never had tea and biscuits before, you know."

"A habit I picked up from my mother. She was from England," she says as she sits down in the recliner opposite me, her own mug cradled in her hands. For a moment, neither of us speaks. The only sounds are the soft crackle of the fire and the faint clink of the teaspoon as she stirs her tea.

It's almost like she's waiting, trying to be polite. Looking at her now, she seems nothing like the woman who'd barged her way into my home and threatened me.

The warmth of the tea seeps into my hands, and I lift the mug to my mouth. It's rich and earthy, with a hint of something floral. It's surprisingly really nice.

Val doesn't drink. She just stares into her mug, her

shoulders tense, her face unreadable. When she finally looks up, her eyes lock onto mine, and the intensity there makes my breath hitch.

"Who killed my son?"

I let out a slow breath, trying to steady my heart. I know she's not going to like what I'm about to say. "I'll tell you, but I need you to do something for me."

The intensity in her gaze ramps up a notch, and her lips pull back over her teeth. I can see it now, just how much she hates me.

"Of course you do," she seethes.

"It's not what you think. It's... personal." This time, it's me who looks down into my mug. "It's about my mother."

She leans back in her chair, her unwavering gaze never leaving me. "She's not well."

I look up at her.

"I heard the sound of medical equipment that day I came into your house. I used to be a nurse. Sounded just like the hospital. What does she have?"

"Locked-In Syndrome."

By the way Val winces, I know she's aware of how rare and serious it is.

"Becoming Miss Murder has only ever been about helping my mother. The money I make is for her." I set my mug down onto the coffee table and lean forward, my eyes pleading. "That's why I need you to withdraw your statement. Make a post, tag me in it, tell everyone that you were mistaken."

Her jaw tightens. "Why the hell would I do that?"

"Because I can't take care of my mother if Miss

Murder's income is destroyed by this," I say bluntly. "And if you don't retract your statement, that's exactly what's going to eventually happen."

Her eyes flash with anger. "So this is about money? About saving your precious brand while my son—"

"No," I cut her off, my voice firm. "It's giving my mother what she deserves, and giving you what *you* deserve."

She blinks, thrown by the last part of my statement. "What?"

"You said it on Momnt. You want justice, right? Real justice?" I lean forward slightly, my voice dropping. "Then let me help you get it. Not through some media circus that ends with lawyers tearing apart every detail until it's impossible to prove anything. Not by dragging me down with you while the real monster gets away. I'm talking about actual justice. The kind that sticks."

Her lips part like she's about to argue, but then she hesitates. I press on before she can interrupt.

"I know who killed your son," I say again, my voice steady. "And I'll give him to you. I'll get you the justice you deserve. But I can't do that if you keep going like this. If Miss Murder falls apart, I can't protect my mother, and I can't help you. We'll both lose."

Her silence stretches on for what feels like forever. Finally, she speaks, her voice quieter now. "And how do I know you're telling the truth? That you *actually* know who the killer is?"

"You don't," I admit. "But if you're willing to trust me, I'll give you what you want. I swear."

Her eyes search mine, and for a moment, I think she's

going to refuse. But then she nods, the motion slow and deliberate.

"Okay, Luna," she says, her voice barely above a whisper. Then she leans forward, her mug of tea still cupped between her hands, and adds, "But if you are lying to me and I find out this is a trick you're playing against me, I'll do what a mother has to do. You understand what I'm saying, right?"

There's a dark look in her eyes. It doesn't take two guesses for me to know that if this doesn't go right, then she'll be the one to kill me. Not Vincent.

I slowly nod.

She sets the mug aside and stands. "I'll tell the book community on Momnt today. Tomorrow, you better make good on your word. Now, let me show you to the door."

She leads me to the door and closes it behind me without another word. It's only when I get back behind the wheel of my car that I draw another breath. But I'm not put at ease yet. There's still so much that can go wrong. And it's not lost on me that I only have *one* chance to pull this off.

Somehow, I have to make it count.

TWENTY-SEVEN

My nails are practically gone, chewed down to raw stubs as I sit in my office, gripping my phone, my leg bouncing with nervous energy. Anxiety twists in my stomach as I refresh Momnt again and again, waiting for Val's tag. The thought of what she could do gnaws at me. She could turn this entire thing around on me with just a single post, spinning my visit into something it wasn't.

The book community would lose their minds. They'd go feral. If they found out that I'd shown up at her house, tried to persuade her to withdraw her statements, they wouldn't just cancel me. They'd annihilate me. The current controversy was nothing compared to what kind of storm *that* would create. There would be people who would show up at my house in retaliation. The thought alone makes me want to pull my hair out.

I should've had Val create the post for me while I was there. At least then, she wouldn't have time to think twice about my promise and wouldn't be tempted to destroy me.

It wouldn't even be that hard to prove it. She could post video footage of me parked out in front of her house for over half an hour. Hell, she could probably just *say* it and people would believe her at this point. And the worst part? I wouldn't even be able to defend myself, because I *was* there.

I glance up at the distant sound of footsteps. That would be Vincent, crossing the hall to my mother's room to check on her and handle any of her needs.

A wondering thought comes to me. Did my mother know what kind of man Vincent really was? Was that what the fear in her eyes meant? God, what was I going to do?

The phone buzzes in my hand, the screen lighting up with a notification from Momnt. My breath hitches as I stare at it, my thumb hovering over the notification like it might explode if I tap it. But I have to. I can't just sit here imagining the worst.

It's Val. She's tagged me. And it's a video.

My chest tightens as I tap the notification, the screen filling with her somber face. The background is her dimly lit living room, the edges of the frame revealing the worn, sagging couch I'd seen earlier. Her hair is pulled back, her expression grim but composed.

"I owe you all an apology," she begins. "These past weeks, I've been speaking out about Luna Harrow—Miss Murder—and the connection between *Don't Breathe Twice* and my son Cody's death. I believed with everything in me that the details in her book were too similar to be coincidence. But I've recently seen proof that I was... wrong."

Her throat works as she swallows hard, her hand tightening into a fist on her lap. "I need to clear it up, on my own good conscience. What lies between *Don't Breathe Twice* and my son's death are not the same. They *are* coincidences. Painful, horrible coincidences, but coincidences nonetheless."

She hesitates, shifting her gaze away from the camera in a way that tugs at my heart.

"I let my grief blind me. I let it fuel my accusations, and in doing so, I dragged an innocent author through the mud. That wasn't right. Luna didn't deserve that. And I'm truly sorry."

She pauses again, this time looking straight into the camera.

"But my promise to my son still stands. Justice will find its way, and *soon*, he'll rest easy knowing the truth has been laid to rest alongside him."

The video ends with her lips pressing into a tight line, as if she can't bring herself to say anything more.

I sit frozen, staring at the screen as the video loops back to the start.

The truth has been laid to rest alongside him.

The veiled threat isn't lost on me. And I certainly don't intend to be the one to fill the grave. Before I can tap to read the comments, I see a new trending hashtag suggested at the top.

#WeStandWithLuna.

Tears come to my eyes, and when I do finally open the comments, I see a flood of people apologising to me, rallying around me in droves as they called me a victim of Val's grief. They're practically crowning me a saint, even going so far as to tag Alyssa Lake everywhere they can.

A sharp breath escapes me as I slump back into my chair. Relief washes over me, but it doesn't feel like the celebration it should be. I glance at my hands, trembling slightly, and clutch them together to steady myself.

I can't let myself be that saint. Not yet. If I want to secure my mother's safety, I'll have to reach inside and find the devil instead.

I push back from the desk, my chair scraping against the floor as I stand. My pulse quickens as I glance toward the closet at the back of the office. The old bat inside, tucked behind the stacks of dusty boxes.

There was no other way to do this. This was the only way.

The bat feels heavier in my hands than I remember, the weight grounding me as I grip it tightly. My fingers tremble, but not from fear. No, this isn't fear anymore. This is purpose. This is resolve.

I creep across the hallway, my breath shallow and measured. It feels like the entire house is holding its breath along with me. The muffled hum of my mother's machines grows louder with each step I take. My heart pounds in my ears, a steady, deafening rhythm, but I don't let it distract me.

The door to her room is cracked open, the warm glow of the bedside lamp spilling into the hallway. I inch closer, peering inside. Vincent is there, his broad back to me as he leans over my mother, adjusting her blanket. His movements are slow, careful, almost tender.

He hums softly, some tune I can't place. His shoulders are relaxed, like he doesn't have a care in the world. I suppose he thinks he doesn't. After all, with the police no longer on his trail, he's free to keep killing. My fingers tighten around the handle of the bat. It's almost laughable, how unaware he is, how oblivious to what's coming.

I take one step inside, the floor shifting faintly beneath me. He doesn't turn. Doesn't even pause.

"Almost done here," he says softly, his voice calm. "Just getting her settled."

A sadness creeps over my heart. Even now, he doesn't suspect me, doesn't know what's about to happen to him.

Beyond him, my mother's eyes are locked onto the ceiling, same as always. They're charged with emotion, my poor mother forever unable to express them to me. But she doesn't have to.

"Don't worry, Mom," I whisper, more to myself than to her. "I've got you."

Vincent straightens.

Now.

I swing.

The bat connects with the back of his head with a sickening thud. His body jerks, then crumples to the floor. For a moment, the only sound in the room is the steady beep of my mother's machines and the rasp of my own breathing.

I bend over my mother, the bat still clutched in one hand. A smear of blood dots her cheek, bright against her pale skin. I set the bat down, my hands trembling as I wipe the blood away with my sleeve.

"It's okay, Mom," I say softly, running a hand gently

over her hair. My voice is steady now, calm. "I've got it handled. You're safe. I promise."

Then I back away from her, grab Vincent's unconscious body by the wrists, and start to drag him away.

The drag to my office is slow, my muscles straining with the weight of his body. I'm not sure why I expected it to be easier, like his body would somehow glide across the hardwood. But instead, it almost feels like he's rooted to it.

Sweat beads along my hairline, my muscles burning with the effort. I have to stop every so often to catch my breath and check to make sure that he's still out cold. The hair along the back of his head is clumped with blood.

I shouldn't feel guilty. He's a serial killer. But even so, there's a knot in my chest that tightens every time I bump him into a wall or doorway. It doesn't matter. Guilt is a luxury I can't afford right now.

When I finally reach the office, I collapse into the chair for just a moment, sucking in air and glancing around the room for something to tie him up with. Rope would've been ideal, but I don't have any. My eyes land on a box in the corner, filled with exercise equipment that I bought and never used. There are some exercise bands in there. That'll have to do.

I kneel down and start binding him to the chair, wrapping the exercise bands tight enough around him that it'll dig into his wrists, ankles, and shoulders. It's not elegant work, but he seems to be secured in place.

Vincent's head lolls to one side, his face slack and peaceful. It's eerie, how normal he looks. Like he could be sleeping. Like he isn't the monster who has been the subject of every one of my reader's obsession for more than two years. He would probably wake up soon. After all, I hadn't hit him *that* hard.

I double check to make sure that I have everything that I need. The typewriter case sits next to my desk, along with Janice's letter as proof. The bat rests against the desk, close enough to grab in case things don't go as I plan, though it would probably be smart to grab a knife.

Satisfied, I grab my phone and scroll to Val's name. We lived far enough apart that it would take her a while to drive here. Better to call her now. I press the dial button and start to head downstairs to get a knife.

The phone rings once. Twice.

When her voice answers, sharp and unyielding, I close my eyes and steady my breath.

"It's me," I say.

There's a pause, the tension crackling through the line like static. "What do you want, Luna?"

"I have him. The man who killed your son."

Silence. And then, in a low and dangerous voice, she answers.

"I'm coming."

TWENTY-EIGHT

It's only twenty minutes later when the doorbell rings. My heart leaps into my throat, and my grip tightens around the bat. I glance out the window and see Val's car in the driveway. She's here.

I check on Vincent, slumped unconscious in the chair, his bindings still secure. Satisfied he isn't going anywhere, I make my way to the door.

The door swings open. Val's eyes are dark, sunken, and her mouth is pressed into a thin, resolute line. But beneath it all, there's something else. Something fragile. Like even now, with everything she's ever wanted within reach, she's bracing herself for it to slip through her fingers. Bracing herself for her son's killer to get away once again. But this time, that wasn't going to happen.

My gaze drops to her purse, clutched tightly in her hands. Her knuckles are white against the leather, and I don't need two guesses to know what's inside.

She takes a step forward, her eyes darting behind me, searching the house. She's looking for him. For Vincent.

"Stop," I say, holding up a hand.

Her brow furrows. "What?"

I nod toward her purse. "Leave that in the car."

Her eyes flick down to the bag, confusion flashing across her face before realization sets in. I can tell she's a little surprised that I know what's inside, though she shouldn't be. She pointed it at me all too recently. "The gun?"

"Yes," I say firmly. "If we want to get away with this, we can't use that. It's too loud. Too messy."

Her expression falters, and for a moment, she looks almost childlike. In her all her dreams, she's probably played this out a thousand times. Pulling the trigger, feeling the recoil, watching the man who killed her son fall to the ground. But that fantasy dies here. I wasn't about to get caught so easily. This had to be done up close and personal, with a knife or bare hands and nothing less.

Her hands tighten around the purse. "You're asking me to—"

"I'm telling you," I cut her off, my voice low and steady. "This has to be quiet. If we do it your way, the neighbors will hear. The cops will come. Everything goes wrong and he gets away. Is that what you want?"

She draws a sharp breath, her chest rising and falling like she's trying to steady herself. She doesn't move, doesn't speak.

"Leave it behind, Val," I say again, softer this time but no less commanding. "Or you're not coming in."

Her eyes meet mine, and for a moment, I think she's going to argue. But then, slowly, she nods. Her hand slips into the purse, and she pulls out the gun. It gleams in the dim light, a cold, lifeless thing. She looks at it for a long moment before turning and walking back to her car.

I exhale, the tension in my chest loosening just enough for me to breathe again. When she comes back, her hands are empty. I can tell she's still not too happy about it.

I shut the door behind her, and she follows me down the hallway. The shadows press in around us, swooping into the places our feet just stepped.

It's strange, too, how even the sound of my mother's equipment is muted. I wait for Val to glance in her direction, like she did that first day she forced her way inside—but she never does. Like me, she must be too caught up in the fact that a killer is waiting just a few steps away.

We reach the door, and I can almost hear how tight her breathing is. I pause, meeting her gaze head-on, waiting for her to calm down. She looks on the edge of hyperventilating, her pupils blown wide and her fists clenched at her sides. Then her eyes flick up to mine, like she's surprised I haven't opened the door yet.

"Take a deep breath," I say.

She does, her fists slowly uncurling, her shoulders loosening.

"I want to make sure we're on the same page of what's going to happen in there," I say, holding her gaze.

"We're going to make sure he's never able to hurt anyone ever again," she says, in response to the question in my eyes.

"You understand that if I open this door, there's no turning back?"

She nods.

"And whatever happens inside, we'll never speak a word about this to anyone. Right?"

"Never." She pauses. "But you're sure you have the right person?"

I nod, slow and certain. "I'm sure."

"How?"

I press a finger to my lips, then open the door. I'd rather just show her.

Val's breath hitches at the sight of Vincent. He's beginning to stir into consciousness, and he softly groans, still too out of it to realize that he's bound to my leather chair.

Val's eyes narrow as she takes him in, like she's trying to summon some glimpse of familiarity—something that would make the death of her son at least make sense. But it won't. The sad truth is, her son was murdered at random. It was him just as easily as it could've been the mailman who drops off our papers every week.

"Who is he?"

I brush past her, heading toward the desk. In a quiet voice, I answer, "He's my mother's caretaker."

Her eyes narrow, catching on the personal connection. I see the flicker of confusion, maybe even suspicion, in her eyes.

I pick up the typewritten note and hand it to her, watching closely as she unfolds it. Her brows furrow deeper with each word, the lines on her face tightening as she struggles to grasp what's in front of her.

"He blackmailed my editor into ghostwriting for me," I say, my voice steady but low. "Made her watch as he murdered people—including your son. Forced her to use that typewriter," I nod toward the case containing the typewriter on the desk, "to turn their deaths into thrillers for me to publish, not knowing what the stories really were."

Her breath stutters. "But why?"

I turn my gaze to him, bound and groaning, the sound growing louder as he stirs. His hand jerks weakly toward his head, straining against the tight bands that hold him in place.

Because he cares for me.

The thought twists in my stomach, nearly making me nauseous. I shove it down, unwilling to let it surface, let alone share it with her. She's already been suspicious of me in the past. Saying something like that would probably do me over.

Instead, I just shrug. "Don't know. But it doesn't matter, does it?"

Vincent's eyes flutter open, half-lidded and confused, like he's trapped in a bad dream. But he's not. This is as real as it gets.

"Luna?" His voice sounds shredded, like it barely made it past his throat. He blinks a few times, gaze ricocheting between me and Val, as though he can't process us both at once.

Val thrusts the letter back into my hand and storms forward, all but trembling with fury. "Look at me."

He does. He gives her a direct, unwavering stare.

"I want to hear you say it," she demands.

"Say what?" he rasps.

She coils her fist and slams it into his jaw with a ragged shriek. It's not the power behind the punch that makes his head whip to the side—it's the sheer shock of it.

He swivels his gaze to me, confusion scrawled across his features. "What's going on?"

Val lunges in, seizing his jaw. Her fingers dig in like claws as she hisses, "Don't pretend you don't know. You killed my son, you bastard."

The accusation is charged with every ounce of her grief.

"You murdered my boy," she repeats, her voice dipping into a lethal quiet that makes me clamp down harder on the baseball bat handle.

Vincent's eyes dart desperately to me. "Luna, I—I didn't—"

But Val is already choking him, her fingers locked around his throat. He flails, trying to yank free of the restraints, but there's no escape.

"Val," I say, my heart hammering.

She doesn't so much as flinch.

"Val!" I shout.

She finally loosens her grip, just enough to let him suck in a ragged breath, then shoots me a glare like I've betrayed her.

"I want to hear him say it first," I tell her, my voice tight with my own brand of anger and heartbreak.

Vincent's gaze snaps to me, incredulous. "Say *what*? What do you want me to say, Luna?"

Val grits her teeth, but she nods at me, perhaps recognizing that I'm no less a victim than she is. He didn't just destroy my present—he murdered the future I had believed in.

I hold up Janice's typewritten letter, letting him see just enough of those damning lines. His eyes flick from the letter to the typewriter case, and when he looks back at me, something in him *shifts*. The version of Vincent I knew peels away, replaced by a dark, gleaming smirk.

"I guess you finally know. But I did it all for you," he whispers.

That's all the confession we need.

Val unleashes a ragged roar and lunges at him, nails biting into his neck until his face starts to turn purple. And even then, his eyes remain locked on me, unblinking, as though he'd gladly die if it meant dying for me.

The veins around his eyes bulge; the light inside them flickers and begins to fade.

He's dying.

Finally.

A hollow, heavy thud cleaves the air. My swing sends Val reeling away from Vincent with a strangled gasp, and then her knees give out, sending her crashing to the floor.

I stand there, bat still poised in my grip, drawing in a slow, deliberate breath. For a moment, the only sound in the world is Vincent's ragged inhalation.

Then, I exhale.

I point the bat at him, my nerves thrumming so loudly I can practically hear them buzz in my skull. Vincent's gaze dances between the bat and Val's limp form on the floor. He's still catching his breath, wrestling with the shock of what I've done.

"Why did you kill Stephen?" I demand in a sharp voice. I can't hold it back any longer. His eyes flick to me, startled.

He hesitates, the cords of his neck straining against the restraints. For a moment, I see regret—or maybe it's shame—but it doesn't last. His face settles into a fractured mix of remorse and devotion.

"Because you wanted him gone," he says, so quietly it's almost a breath.

"All because you thought I wanted it," I say, my voice trembling. "So you killed him."

He nods, a sick worship gleaming behind his eyes. "Everything was for you. Always."

My heart pounds harder.

"Then why did you take everything from me?" I whisper, stepping closer.

"What?"

"My dream. My book. The chance to write something real. You should've never let Janice take over my stories. You fed her your twisted ideas—your murders—and she never had to imagine a single thing. She never had to struggle for the words herself. And me?" I choke on a bitter laugh. "I just got left behind. You should never have done that, Vincent. You should have trusted me, instead of ripping me away from my *own* dream."

Vincent's gaze flicks over me, and I see it: he's equally enthralled and terrified. He must see it now, how he's done everything wrong, all in the name of doing it for me.

"I was trying to help you."

"Is that so?" I ask with an ugly snarl. I prod his chest with the tip of the bat. A molten energy swirls inside my head, like the bars of my mind have been pried open, letting in colors and shapes I never could've imagined. "Then this is your one chance to fix it. Show me how far you'll go, Vincent. Be my inspiration. Give *me* something real to write."

He just stares, uncomprehending.

My bat hovers in the direction of Val, her body sprawled on the floor, chest still faintly rising and falling.

"Kill her," I say, the words spilling out like poison and honey at once. My breath hitches. "Kill her and I'll write it. It'll be my book—my masterpiece—written from the blood you spill."

His eyes widen, adrenaline coursing through him like a fever. "Luna..." He sounds rattled, but beneath that, there's a flicker of dark fascination. He wants to please me.

"You say you did all of this for me," I press, letting the tip of the bat rest on Val's shoulder. "Then prove it. *Inspire* me."

For a heartbeat, his gaze shifts to Val, then back to me. Something unhinged passes through his expression. He gives the restraints an eager tug, like he's begging to be set free so he can do exactly what I've asked.

I swallow hard. There's a hollow pit in my stomach, but an electric heat buzzes in my veins. A spark of creativity—of actual, unfiltered imagination—roars to life in my mind. I can almost see the words forming in the air before me, the scene writing itself in real-time.

She's still breathing, I think distantly, my heart stuttering. Do I really want to do this?

I draw another breath, and it comes easier than any before.

"Yes," I whisper, barely louder than my own pulse. I lift my gaze to Vincent's. He inhales a ragged breath. His lips curve into the same twisted smirk that first broke through when I confronted him with Janice's letter. I see the mania glint in his eyes—the same mania that killed Stephen just because I wanted him gone. The same mania that killed Janice when he must have realized the threat she posed to us both.

"Do this," I repeat, forcing the words out through trembling lips, "and all that will leave this room are me, you, and the pages I fill."

Vincent's breathing turns shallow as he readies himself. I stand there, bat in hand, my heart pounding in my chest, waiting for the moment that will shatter the last thread of decency I have.

He's about to paint me a story in blood, and for the first time, I can actually see it in my mind.

I'm finally ready to write.

I free Vincent from the restraints, letting the bands fall to the floor. He staggers to his feet, eyes locked on me in something akin to worship. The bat remains in my grip, knuckles white against the taped handle, until I press it into his waiting palms.

Then, I settle in at the desk and open the typewriter case. A blank page lies there, like it was just waiting for a story. My pulse jumps with excitement as I rest my fingers on the silent keys, and I can't help but wonder... was this how Janice felt every time she sat down to write?

Vincent stands before me, weapon in hand, gaze darting from me to Val. She's still sprawled on the floor, unconscious—maybe barely clinging to life. The faint rise and fall of her chest is almost imperceptible, but it's enough to draw him in. I sense him shift—a drawn breath, the subtle give of weight—like a predator about to close in on its prey.

My heart hammers.

Vincent raises the bat above his head, dark eyes gleaming, and with one last look at me, he brings it down with a sickening crack.

Blood spatters onto the typewriter, onto my fingers, onto my face, and rips a ragged scream from my lungs. But that scream twists into something exhilarating, something that urges me to press the keys. The carriage of the typewriter snaps each letter into place like a pulsing drumbeat.

The words come slowly at first, but *they come*.

I hear Val's low, broken moan. My pulse falters, but not from horror. It's something else, coiling deep in my chest, demanding that I pour these words onto the page—faster and faster.

My writing explodes in a frantic rush I've never felt before, and Vincent must sense it too, because he raises the bat again and again. His breathing turns ragged, punctuated by Val's strangled gasps, and then the wet, feral impact of wood on flesh.

I feel the heat of it wash over me, a primal thrill like a thousand sparks firing in my brain, each one birthing another phrase, another sentence—a paragraph drenched in such beautiful brutality.

The room reeks of copper and panic, but my exhilaration only intensifies. I'm drunk on it, on the raw reality unfolding just behind me. For the first time, I don't have to worry about my aphantasia; the story practically writes itself, word after word, as easy as Val's own death.

A mocking voice echoes in my head—my old teacher's voice.

You'll never write anything real.

I pause for half a heartbeat, and laugh. If only Mr. Thompson could see me now. The typewriter's return bell dings, begging for the next line. I stare at the half-finished page, chest heaving with the aftershocks of adrenaline. Vincent's breath hitches, and I meet his gaze.

A dark smile blooms across my face; he answers it in kind. Then, I press the next key. And the next. And the next.

Because this is *mine*—*my* story, *my* dream, written into existence by the horror and devotion bound together in this room. Call me mad, psycho, whatever you want; no matter what, I know I'll never again have to worry about that blinking cursor. And I know this will not only be a book my fans devour, but it will be better than *any* that came before. Better than even Janice's books.

The muted sound of my mother's equipment drones on in the room down the hall, and my smile inches wider, because this is the first time I've written something.

And I can't wait to read it to her.

EPILOGUE

My ears are ringing with applause before I even step on stage. There are a record number of viewers tuning in for the explosive segment of *The Truth About Miss Murder*, heightened only by the fact that late last night, I chose to hit 'publish' on my newest release, *Keep Your Lies*.

The release sent shockwaves across the internet, and when I woke up this morning to get dressed for Alyssa Lake's show, it seemed that everybody had already read it.

I had been right.

They loved this book more than any before. The Momnt community was screaming over it with a fervor none of my books had matched before, calling it raw, daring, the kind of story that sank its claws in them and never let go.

I can't help but smile as I look across the stage at Alyssa Lake, knowing that I had disrupted whatever plans she'd had for the show. For once, she wasn't in control. I was.

Her assistant taps me on the shoulder and leans in, telling me to get ready. After a soft count, I hear Alyssa's voice boom, reaching the ears of millions of viewers.

"Please welcome, the author behind last night's most explosive release, the creator and mastermind behind *Keep Your Lies*, Luna Harrow, or as you all know her, Miss Murder!"

The studio crowd goes wild, cheering in that way only a live audience can—equal parts adrenaline and curiosity. Cameras glide across the stage, capturing the moment from every angle; the moment that I own as I walk confidently across the stage toward Alyssa Lake, feeling more myself than ever. I match her signature grin, and when she extends her hand, I take her firm grip in mine. Except when she meets my eyes, she sees something in them that makes her grip soften just enough for me to feel.

I swear I see her swallow as she gestures to the white chair. I take my seat, cross my legs, and give a soft wave to the crowd. The crowd cheers again, this time the sound so deafening that even Alyssa has to pull back. She gives a sharp whistle.

"It would seem, Luna, that you are America's darling!"

Cheers flare up once more, and I give the slightest tilt of my head, an almost bashful smile.

"Before we dive into any controversies," Alyssa continues, one leg crossing over the other, "I have to congratulate you. This new book? This new *you*? It's like I'm talking to someone who's been reborn!"

The audience laughs and applauds, and my stomach

tightens with satisfaction. If only they all knew how true that was.

"You're not the first person to say that," I answer, leaning into the plush couch. The stage lights are sweltering, but in the best way. Like a spotlight shining just for me. "I guess I've... tapped into something new."

"New is an understatement," Alyssa exclaims, crossing one leg over the other. "Online reviews are pouring in. And the Momnt community is going ballistic over *Keep Your Lies*. Readers say it's *better* than anything you've ever done—that it was positively haunting. Most found it impossible to put down." She tosses her hair back and grins. "And, if I may be honest, that includes me. It's bold to release it the night before you walk across this stage. I guess that's maybe why I see so many sleepy faces out there!"

A ripple of laughter spreads through the studio, and I let myself bask in the glow for a moment. My cheeks warm with gratitude and pride.

"That means a lot," I say, fighting to keep my voice steady under the rush of adrenaline. "I poured everything into this one."

"Oh, we can tell," she answers with a conspiratorial wink. "But let's be honest: this show isn't just about celebrating your latest masterpiece—though it definitely deserves the fanfare." She turns to address the audience directly. "We're here for a segment called *The Truth About Miss Murder*, because there were some pretty outrageous rumors flying around about our beloved author here—rumors tying her last book, *Don't Breathe Twice*, to a supposed, shall we say, superfan."

Some in the audience begin to boo.

Alyssa arches an eyebrow, voice full of practiced drama. "Of course, it turned out to be an unfortunate lie—just a grieving mother who thought she'd take Luna down with her. But we haven't heard how Luna handled it." She swivels back to me with an earnest expression, as if she truly cares. "Luna, I can't imagine how painful it must have been to see something like that blow up."

Painful? I almost scoff, but I catch myself. Instead, I lean forward, letting my face melt into a carefully measured look of vulnerability. Because Alyssa Lake wants a show—and I'm more than happy to give it to her.

"It wasn't easy," I say with a faint sigh, forcing a trace of uncertainty into my voice. "That's part of why *Keep Your Lies* meant so much to me. It's about pushing through, holding on until you find that perfect spark—one that... *inspires* you and changes everything."

Alyssa nods, her eyes gleaming like we're sharing some wonderful secret. For a heartbeat, the studio lights seem to glow hotter, reflecting off her hair, and the crowd's hush feels electric. Everyone is waiting for the next revelation.

But as far as I'm concerned, *I've* already had my revelation. And I don't plan on sharing it with anybody.

The camera zooms in, capturing every nuance of my expression, every flicker of meaning that dances behind my eyes. And in that moment, I realize I've never felt more alive. Or more seen.

"Believe me, Luna," Alyssa murmurs, leaning in for that final dramatic hook, "we're all dying to know what lit that spark for you."

I let a thin smile curve across my lips, keeping the tension crackling in the studio for just one more heartbeat. Because, in truth, I own this moment—and everything that's about to follow.

"Well," I say, my voice slipping out in a cool rush, "I guess you'll have to read my next book to find out. It'll be coming out soon."

The crowd explodes with thunderous applause at the prospect of another release so quickly. Alyssa grins wide for the cameras, but I know she must be burning behind that smile—she's aware I've hijacked her stage and bent it to my own plans.

She tries to pivot to her closing remarks, but the audience is already on its feet, roaring their approval. They want to praise me for the torment they think I suffered, and more than that, they want to devour the next novel I've promised them.

Alyssa forces a laugh, playing the part of the good sport, while my own smile shines genuine as I rise, placing a hand over my heart in acknowledgement of my fans. Then I turn and stride off stage, heels tapping a soft staccato against the polished floor. Behind me, Alyssa follows a few beats later, the raucous applause still crashing through the studio.

"I must say, Luna," she says once we're out of earshot, "that was masterfully done."

The applause fades as the stage lights begin to dim, and Alyssa steps closer, her heels clicking softly against the polished floor. Her expression shifts—less polished, more piercing—as she studies me like she's seeing something she hadn't noticed before.

"*Keep Your Lies,*" she says quietly, her voice low enough that only I can hear it. "It's different from the others, isn't it? This one... you actually wrote it yourself."

The words land cleanly, sharply, like she's testing me, waiting for a reaction. My lips curve into a slow, deliberate smile. There's no nervousness in me anymore, no trembling doubt. Alyssa has no idea what she's really just said—or what it might mean for her.

"I suppose it is," I reply, the corners of my mouth lifting ever so slightly. "It's amazing what you can create when you're truly... inspired."

Her head tilts, that sharp, television-ready grin softening into something far more dangerous: curiosity. It lingers in the air as she studies me a moment longer. Then she extends her hand.

"Keep it up, Miss Murder," she says, her voice laced with a strange mix of approval and challenge.

I take her hand, my grip firm, watching as her gaze lingers a second too long before she turns and strides down the hall, heels echoing into silence.

Maybe she will be the inspiration for my next book.

The thought curls around me like smoke as I step outside into the cool night air. Vincent waits in the car, his silhouette half-lit by the amber glow of a streetlamp. He glances my way as I approach, his expression calm, patient—almost like he already knows what's on my mind.

I slide into the passenger seat and shut the door, the faint scent of ink lingering in the air between us.

For a moment, neither of us speaks. Something dark

and intimate passes between us—something that doesn't need words to be understood.

As the car rumbles to life, I glance over at him.

I wonder, just for a moment, if I'll ever be a Mrs. Murder.

The city lights blur into streaks as we glide into the night, the studio fading into the rearview mirror. That familiar thrill stirs deep inside me—creation, clawing at the edges of my mind, words waiting to burst free.

Another book is coming.

A LETTER FROM ZIA

Dear Reader,

If you've made it to this point... you survived!

Thank you so much for reading Miss Murder. Writing this book was an unbelievable amount of fun, and I hope it kept you on the edge of your seat until the very last page.

If you enjoyed the story, the best thing you can do is leave an honest review. Not for me (though yes, I do read every one), but for fellow readers who want to know what they're stepping into. Your thoughts help this book reach the people who'll love it most.

And if you'd like to reach out directly, I'd love to hear from you. Whether you're Team Miss Murder or still deciding if you trust her, shoot me a message at zia.rayyan.author@gmail.com. I personally respond to every note—because stories connect us, but it's the readers who bring them to life.

Until next time,
Zia

ALSO BY ZIA RAYYAN

Miss Murder
Mrs. Murder
The Newlywed

ABOUT THE AUTHOR

Zia Rayyan is a psychological thriller author with no background, no alibi—only a need to write about the lies we tell, and the ones we bury.

You can reach Zia at ziarayyan.com or by email at zia.rayyan.author@gmail.com.

You may also see Zia being quite active in the Psychological Thriller Readers Facebook group—come join the community. But only if you can keep a secret.

Made in the USA
Columbia, SC
22 June 2025